DEALER'S WHEELS

Steve Wilson

Macmillan

ISBN 0 333 32232 0

First published 1982 by
MACMILLAN LONDON LIMITED
London and Basingstoke
Associated companies in Auckland, Dallas, Delhi,
Dublin, Hong Kong, Johannesburg, Lagos, Manzini, Melbourne,
Nairobi, New York, Singapore, Tokyo,
Washington and Zaria

Typeset in Great Britain by
MB GRAPHIC SERVICES LIMITED
Bovingdon, Hertfordshire

Printed in Great Britain by
THE ANCHOR PRESS LIMITED
Tiptree, Essex

Bound in Great Britain by
WM. BRENDON AND SON LIMITED
Tiptree, Essex

... if the noxious particles that rise from vitiated air were palpable to the sight, we should see them lowering in a dense black cloud above such haunts, and rolling slowly on to corrupt the better portions of the town. But if the moral pestilence that arises from them, and, in the eternal lows of outraged Nature, is inseparable from them, could be made discernible too, how terrible the revelation!

Charles Dickens, *Dombey and Son*

'What is it like?'
'Well, it's always cold. It's always lonely. It's always dark – even in the daytime, it always seems to be dark.'

A British Army bomb-disposal officer in
Ulster, interviewed by BBC TV

The author and publishers wish to thank the following who have kindly given permission for the use of copyright material:

EMI Music Publishing Limited, London, for an extract from the song *Whatever's Written in Your Heart* by Gerry Rafferty. ©1977 Gerry Rafferty.

Faber and Faber Limited, for an extract from *The Waste Land* in *Collected Poems 1909-1962* by T. S. Eliot.

PROLOGUE

I was back in London, living in an attic in Barnsbury on Chinese take-away and amphetamines.

I had a straight job, working as a van driver for a courier firm; when it had really come to Death Before Employment, my loyalty to the slogan had crumbled. That day it was early February; the time was around half past four in the afternoon, and I was between calls. The outfit I worked for was a small one, not radio-controlled, and dealing mostly in the City and West End, so when I had to hang about between jobs a favourite place was around Holborn Viaduct Station; midway between those two areas, never too busy, with meter parking close by around Smithfield Market and plenty of phones in the station that worked. There were newsagents and a smattering of pubs and cafés round about, to serve the postmen from the big post office and typists from the legal offices around the Old Bailey and from Bart's Hospital opposite it, just down Giltspur Street.

It was also a short step down the wide, dirty, covered stairs that descended in a brick tunnel beside the maroon and gold viaduct road bridge itself into Farringdon Street below, and the place where I drank: a small Fleet Street pub which consequently opened at five o'clock, half an hour earlier than elsewhere, with a clientele of printers from the offices of the papers opposite and, again, a phone that worked.

But that day it was too early for the pub, and I had a small chore to take care of. I was still messing around in a desultory way with painting and drawing, and in the late summer and autumn I had spent some time with my sketch-book in St Sepulchre's churchyard on the corner opposite Holborn Viaduct Station, the Welsh Guard's memorial gardens, trying to get the scene opposite down on paper; in the foreground the

7

hamburger bar on the corner, the crowds scurrying and the traffic roaring away from the lights, and behind them looming the monumental structure of the Old Bailey itself. I always worked slowly and reluctantly and only now, months later, had I got to the point of returning with the nearly finished painting that had resulted from the sketches, and squaring it up with at least the architectural reality — the light and details naturally had changed by now — before putting the finishing touches to it.

It had been a mild winter and that February day was no exception. I was able to enter the gardens and sit on one of the benches, which were now empty both of the secretaries in light dresses who had taken their sandwiches there to sit under the trees at lunchtime in the summer and of the bleary or insensible cider-swigging bums who, though not so seasonal, weren't there that evening. I guessed the ghosts of the Welsh Guardsmen would have approved of both the good-looking girls and the serious drinking. I sat in the chilly twilight of the slightly misty evening and stared at the crossroads. Despite the noise of the traffic revving up and pulling away at the lights of the junction where Newgate Street intersected with Giltspur Street and crossed it to become the viaduct, after a while it seemed a curiously abstracted scene — the mist softening, blurring the streetlights, cafés closing up, and the figures hurrying towards the station with only their moving bodies present; their minds already would be well down the line and home. The light failing, the cars just passing through, the people only half there and the buildings looming behind, the courts and the cathedral, representing perhaps stricken ideas, ideals.

And yet with all that insubstantiality, there was also a strong London flavour to the scene; partly from the smell of the hazy city evening, partly from the individual figures in the landscape: now, waiting to cross the road, a rat-nosed man carrying wrapped in brown paper the sharp triangular shape of a saw; on the other side a tall City of London policeman, his head in the helmet with its ornate crest bending to speak to the paper-seller on the corner, whose billboard that night read, 'CITY COUNCIL CLOSES 5 WCS' — the spending cuts were biting where it really hurt now — and partly the buildings themselves, the squared-off stone, green dome and silhouetted blindfold statue of the Bailey which I could see, and the knowledge of the fineness of Bart's just off to the left, St Paul's beyond, and the curve of Snow Hill behind; its bow-fronted police station stood on the site of the old Saracen's Head Inn where Dickens had had bad old Squeers lodge and Nicholas Nickleby set out for the north. I had discovered this when I'd been half asleep in the car on a meter down there one day and dozily picked out the words 'Saracen's Head' on the parapet of a building further down the hill, and then realized I'd been reading about it the night before. As so often previously, the city seemed for me alive with a subterranean system of coincidence, invisible but as tangible as the Underground in its effects; but whose existence I only grudgingly acknowledged, as curiously this seemed a condition of keeping the system in operation. From notes in my paperback I'd also found that, in Dickens's time, Farringdon Street beneath the viaduct had been a river running down into the Thames; and that Newgate prison had stood where the Old Bailey did now, and that they had publicly hanged prisoners outside until just a little over a hundred years ago, with people crowding out of the windows of the pub opposite, eating and drinking as they watched.

The last to be executed had been an Irishman, a Fenian; which was apt, as there was an IRA active service unit on trial in No. 2 Court at that moment. Some evenings, sitting in the pub in Farringdon Street you could hear the hysterical jangle of bells as police cars, their bubble-gum machines revolving wildly, cleared a swathe on the wrong side for the long blue prison wagon with tiny barred windows that took the men to and from the Bailey; evidently they switched routes whenever they could.

The Irish were on trial for a bombing campaign during the

previous autumn; car-bombs had hit some barracks and a Cabinet Minister's house had gone up in smoke. Before they'd been caught I'll confess to being absurdly, given the odds, but considerably rattled by it all, walking stiffly past cars parked on double lines in likely venues. I'm cowardly by nature anyway, and was then afraid that a negative aspect of that city coincidence might just blow me away — because, having survived some of the situations I had done, to get liquidized by a random terrorist explosion struck me as just the sort of rough justice fate was in the habit of gleefully handing out. At the Old Bailey I felt safe; there had been a big bomb there some years ago and as everyone knows lightning never strikes twice. But I was not too sorry that the boyos had been picked up and were getting their wrists judicially slapped across the road; though there were a lot of discreetly armed Old Bill about in the doorways and on the street corners for that reason, which for me was never a comfortable feeling either.

I was just finishing up and thinking it was time to call the office again and, if there was nothing to do, cut down to the drinker on Farringdon Street, when a sound arrested my attention. I always kept an eye and an ear open for motorbikes, being what used to be called an enthusiast and is now known as a bike freak; and in all the discreet whirring and whizzing of Japanese commuter machinery, this sound stood out like a piranha in a goldfish bowl. It was unmistakably the soulful wail of a British triple, which by its screeching roar had just put its rev counter needle into the red and dumped cork from a standstill. My head jerked up and in a second I saw it, the maroon and white of a big T160 Triumph Trident whipping from the inside lane of Newgate Street at the side of the Bailey, jumping a red light as it hurled in a right turn across the nose of a still stationary Rolls-Royce with a police car behind it and, in a blare of horns from the cross-traffic, it tore past me into Giltspur Street and, engine note mounting, howled off in the direction of Bart's.

I was on my feet and breathless, and not just at the lunacy

of the driving; I had realized in an instant that I knew the bike's rider. Despite a full-face helmet and the speed at which he had shot past, I could have sworn that the rider was an old friend of mine; a good friend and a guy I hadn't seen in years, but who I'd been talking and thinking about just the week before. There is a Magic London, and it seemed to be working overtime.

So I was standing there thinking that when it happened. A rose of flame blossomed from the Rolls-Royce and one heart-stopping second later a deafening thundercrash hit my ears and something picked me up and slammed me back against the wall behind. In that moment before, it seemed in silence, like the time just before a car crash, I had seen the Rolls go up on two wheels, blown towards the car next to it in the outside lane, its metal shell no longer impermeable, shiny and immaculate, but beginning to blur, to expand like a plastic bag filling with water, streamers of smoke and a deadly blurred hail of flying glass blowing from the heart of flame. I saw a policeman on the corner, both feet off the ground, beginning to go down like a skittle, people frozen, open-mouthed.

Then came the excruciating roar. My heart stopped and then I hit hard and slid down the wall, winded, with my hands, too late, over my ears, a hot wind fanning my face like an oven door opening and the tinkle and smack of shrapnel and glass hitting in all directions. I lay where I fell and saw what was left of the Rolls in flames, half on top of the car that had been next to it. Behind it the police car had lost its windscreen, and writhing figures inside clutched bloody faces. Windows were out in the hamburger place, and the bodies of people lay in the road and on the pavements all about. I got myself up. The noise alone was horrible, people sobbing, shrieking, screaming, groaning, a car horn jammed on, the flames wreathing the Rolls licking and crackling until moments later there came a second dull explosion as its petrol ignited and blew the back end off the other car; a thick black column of smoke billowed up against the evening sky. The policeman who had been closest was lying in a puddle and he wasn't moving; one on the other side, blood streaming from his nose, mouth and ears, was trying to claw his way up a wall and stand, but there was a shocking asymmetry to him as one foot was gone. Blasted, cut, crushed and burned, people lay on the pavement screaming, moaning. Dust fell and there was an acrid smell, burning paint and oil and something else, drifting in the thickening air.

I reached the gates of the churchyard. The sound of ambulance bells from St Bartholomew's was starting up, and police and people from the courts were running to help. I ran limping past them in the opposite direction, back down Snow Hill, and beyond the police station reached my van. As I fumbled the keys into the lock and slid behind the familiar wheel, more running figures pounded past. Ears ringing, my head was filled with the thought that if it was Denny I didn't want to know. I switched on, revved, slammed into gear and screeched out from the bay and away, narrowly missing an ambulance coming the other way, swinging up the hill heeled right over on its springs, lights and bells going. I realized my painting was still lying where it had fallen in the churchyard. The scene of old London had been ripped apart. The thoughts were jammed in my head making me grip and shake the wheel. If it was Denny, how the hell could he have done it?

PART ONE

Unreal City
Under the brown fog of a winter dawn,
A crowd flowed over London Bridge, so many,
I had not thought death had undone so many.

T. S. Eliot, *The Waste Land*

Chapter 1

I had been in London for eight months.

The place where I had been living hidden up in South America had come unstuck very suddenly. Out in the camp, the countryside to the west of Argentina where I had been working on an *estancia*, the country's political upheavals had not intruded much. Until a couple of summers back, when the son of a local family, a university student, had disappeared in the city. For over a year his family had heard nothing. Finally Robert, my friend and employer at the *estancia*, needing to visit the capital on business, had told the parents that he would ask the authorities about the boy. After two weeks, this time we had heard nothing from Robert. The foreman phoned his hotel; there was no record of him.

With his right-on temperament and 'black humours', one could rough out a guess at what had happened. Such things were not unusual in that anguished, violent country. But the indisputable fact was that, if Robert had disappeared, then it was time for me to do so as well. The government agents would be sniffing around his business, and my irregular situation (no work-permit for a start) would surely come to light. So I went clean-shaven like the picture in my (forged) British passport, tapped into the small sum I had saved from my wages for a scene like this and, with the Andean winds gusting around my newly smooth jowls, crossed the mountains by bus from Bariloche and went over the border into Chile. At a little hotel in Puerto Baras I stared out over the lake and looked for the first time in several years at the electric lights of an urban landscape; a sparse but still arresting return to civilization. And its discontents.

The next day I caught a plane from Santiago to Mexico City; and from there travelled north by bus, a clapped and rattling hand-me-down ex-Greyhound, to cross the border at Nuevo Laredo and enter the great Estados Unidos. From there a pukka Greyhound bus ticket got me to New York. As we approached the city on the New Jersey turnpike through the extraordinary industrial swamp that rings the glittering metropolis, in a car travelling steadily alongside us a young moustached guy looked me directly in the eyes and lazily gave me the peace sign, and I felt something stir that had been dormant literally for years. At JFK I queued for the cheapest Transatlantic stand-by flight, and ten hours later, as evening fell, I was standing in Hackney, on the doorstep of the only guy in London I could trust, a middle-aged dentist named Freddy.

My situation was equivocal. I had fled the country nearly ten years before after a lethal skirmish with some London heavies due to a bit of business about some drugs I'd been dealing at the time; lethal for most of them, that is, but that did not mean they might not have friends still with long memories. The only time I had been back in England since was during another violent go-round with some members of one of the five New York Mafia families. Once more, at the cost of a good friend's life and losing a girl I cared for, most of them had died and I had got clear; but again that didn't mean they wouldn't still have well-wishers who believed in taking care of business.

So coming back to London didn't look to be the best of sense. But aside from a certain fatalism which the above events had planted in me and the Argentine attitude to life had nourished, I did discover in myself a powerful desire to come back home, which meant London. And where else could I go? The States were an even worse bet, and over the past years I'd had a bellyful of neo-colonialism. Aside from which I was broke, and not as young as I had been. Despite the risk, home ways looked like best ways. And if what I felt could be construed as some kind of warped version of patriotism, well, they do say it's the last resort of scoundrels.

But I definitely didn't want to get back in the life, and the drug scene; as I said, I was getting on, in my middle thirties now, and I reckoned I had lost all my taste for adventures the last time, after my friend Dan had been killed. Also hanging out around the old faces would be the quickest way to come into contact with unfriendly elements, as well as the law. So, like the poor immigrant, I arrived on Freddy's doorstep in need of a straight job and a place to live, for openers. And my tooth-pulling friend came through, finding me the Barnsbury attic and my courier work – the landlady and the guv'nor were both patients of his – before succumbing to a mild coronary and disappearing into hospital for a while, leaving me to face the wicked city as best as I could on my own.

My room was an attic on the top floor of a medium-dilapidated house standing on a short piece of unmade road in the corner of quiet square in Barnsbury, full of chestnut trees and derelict motors. The first time I went there to have a look at it was a bright morning in June. The sun was shining, but the night before it had rained heavily; and as I walked up to the house, past a wall which a graffiti artist named Ranking Peanut had made his own, I watched a little girl from the house next door playing in the water in the shingle gutter with a dented ping-pong ball and a toy plastic shovel. Her brother was intermittently bashing an old London taxi-cab with a hammer, not a toy one either, until their mother came out and yelled at him, 'Stop it, Derek! Dad hasn't sold that one yet.'

When I got inside, the flat was just right. There were damp patches on the slanting ceiling by the windows, there was fungus in the bathroom, and the kitchen was so narrow that you couldn't get a tray through the door even sideways. But it was good enough for serving up Chinese take-away from Highbury Corner or making bacon sandwiches; and the windows of my room looked out the back, past a tall chestnut tree down into a big area of back gardens. It was quiet, and had a warm gas fire, and wasn't too expensive. There was no phone, but I couldn't have afforded one anyway, and there weren't that many people I could ring.

And every lonely fellow needs a room; somewhere to stare at the ceiling, work, weep, make notes, pick his toes, read poetry and bring girls: all those things every creature of the twilight must have a place to do. Those first summer evenings after work it was not unpleasant at all to have a wash or a bath and then sit down with a glass of wine on the bed with my back to the wall, looking out through the low open windows over the gardens at the back, with the soft light filtering through the leaves of the chestnut tree where you could hear pigeons cooing, settling for the night.

I liked the area, too; the square's slightly low-rent air was comfortable but, with the district gentrifying apace, not as monotonously oppressive as rougher places further east, across the Holloway Road or down Ball's Pond Road, might have been; it was a frontier, like Notting Hill had been in the sixties when that had been my patch.

And I did need a base in every sense, because both me and the town had got different since I had been away. To begin with, compared with Latin America the city had seemed to be running like clockwork, but before long my inner eye was comparing it to the place I had grown up in. This London was shabbier, and smelt of fast food; clocks on public buildings were stopped, bollards left knocked askew and the state of the roads wasn't far from the battle-field corrugation that had appalled me on the taxi ride to the airport through New York. The drivers, too, seemed to have changed, being markedly less genteel than previously, which led to some sweaty moments till I got in the swing again. The notion that Brits *en masse* were the most polite people in the world seemed to have gone down the tubes along with the idea that they were the greatest. Now, rather than celebrating its existence, London seemed to be just getting by.

The way it hit me most was the girls. Of course, my first sight of punks was a big culture-shock, but, even after I'd got used to that, it seemed the town was staffed entirely with

18

skinny, lippy bisexuals, and contempt or indifference was now the rule as a response to my spaniel-eyed search, on and off the streets, for a friendly female face or some sexual comfort. A lot of it was straight age; like the man said, they just kept getting younger, and prettier every day. But the truth was also that I was well out of style, both superficially, and inside too. The new lot seemed to get off on lots of flash and money, to go for artificial things, glitter, henna, outrageous make-up and disco-poop, in contrast to the long straight hair, faded denim and shit-kicking r and b of my formative years. You've got to remember I had come quite abruptly on a change that had been going on for five or six years; at bottom I knew both styles were dreams, but they were different ones, and I called the one I was familiar with, real. The net result was that at thirty-five I found I was already dwelling on, idealizing, the old days.

The young guy in the flat downstairs went around in an old mac done up with string, a collarless shirt, green RAF overall trousers with a lot of zips, and ratty old plimsolls; his neck was very visible as was his one earring because his black hair sat in glistening curls on top of his head, I think Brylcreemed. I soon got to know him and he turned out to be a nice guy, very obliging and open, since nothing seemed to matter much to him. One day after I'd forced myself past the price-barrier and bought a new pair of jeans, I met him on the stairs and displayed my purchase, but his face contorted in uncontrollable revulsion and he cried, 'Eeeaough! Flares!'

It was the authentic voice of the new. I sulked for a while but next day, ever the trimmer, sneaked out and changed them for eighteen-inch straights. Leather jackets seemed to be OK, so later I bought a black biker's one, and black Doc Martens boots. As an afterthought I grew a short beard again and had my hair cut at no more than collar-length. Like that I felt comfortable and not too *démodé* on the street. It was all right for work too.

Chapter 2

The courier firm I worked for was the brain-child of a guy we called Blithers; passably well-off, an Old Etonian, and younger than me – that was three strikes against him. He had short hair too, but it was the original squash-player's variety – he seemed to have missed the intervening period altogether. He had a habit of blinking a lot, at the same time as talking very fast and hard with what he thought of as executive-type decisiveness but which more often came over as simply ill-considered haste; the combination of the blinks and the blather was presumably where he got his name.

So there was this clown, and Deborah the girl in the office who answered the phones and ran things in a quiet way, me doing pick-ups and deliveries around London and a pool of drivers to-ing and fro-ing long distance. Some of the deliveries were overseas, and to me as an ex-dealer it seemed like a sweet way to move stuff; but when I suggested to Blithers that this might happen, he replied loftily that it was out of the question as all the clients were highly respectable firms and besides, they had all signed a bit of paper saying they wouldn't. Well, ask a silly question.

Deborah's sweet telephone voice had to undo his abruptness with the clients. She was a nice-natured girl in her mid-twenties, with spiky blonde punk hair, a full figure and a young face, innocent-seeming – she talked about home and her parents a lot – but not stupid. The first time I saw her lush body I thought, baby, if you got the curves, I got the angles; but working with someone sort of takes the edge off all that, and anyway she was living with some geezer across the water in Stockwell. But from time to time the boss's verbal excesses would drive the two of us into the pub together – like the Walter Matthau character in *King Creole*, everything he touched turned to drink.

As an employer he was the capricious sort, who rather than pay you a decent wage would do you favours which depended on his mood (though at first the money had seemed all right to me, until it had really sunk in what had happened to the price of everything). In my case, sometimes he would let me use the van over the weekend. That was OK, and also I tried to remind myself that things could have been a lot worse. Before Freddy put me on to Blithers I had looked into the possibility of working for a motorcycle messenger firm; and I hadn't yet forgotten what I had seen when I went round there – the sharp-faced dispatchers and the room full of riders, hopeless-looking red-eyed figures, a couple with torn anoraks sprouting stuffing just like the old car seats they were sitting slumped on around the wall. No thanks.

The business with the van was crucial. Whoever you were, the city streets by now were neither pleasant, convenient or particularly safe places to be on foot; public transport was mostly an expensive joke and wheels were the way out. There was no way I could afford to buy, insure and run a car, so after a couple of months of Blithers's erratic largess, I broke a rule, travelled south of the river and east by train, and looked up an old acquaintance.

Have you ever noticed how mechanics are always a mono-syllable – Len, Perce, Fred, Bert, Jim? Sid was no exception. I walked from the station and squeezed through the complicated doors of his side-street shop and garage, where a tall counter dotted with sliced-off piston-tops for ashtrays separated you from a cave-like unwindowed area behind. It was characteristic that Sid, a short, stocky figure with greasy greying hair, showed no surprise at seeing me for the first time in nearly ten years and that, by the time I had got my attention off both the dim shapes of the bikes in the back and Sid's spectacularly bad teeth, he was already launched into a long, complicated and obscene piece of personal history involving a leaking sewage main outside his house.

'There's turds, see, and rats popping out of nowhere – we got the lot, Jack. It's so bad, yesterday I rang the 'erbs at the

Council and I asks for the gynaecological officer. The gynaecological officer, they say? What you want him for? To find out about cunts, I say, the ones who should be fixing me sewage ...'

After about twenty minutes of this type of stuff which he continued blithely even when customers came in, I gradually worked the conversation around to bikes, observing, 'Sid, I wanted to pick your brains –'

'Bring your tweezers did you?' he interrupted but I went on.

'You're still into British iron. Thought you might have gone under to Jap crap while I was away.'

'If I *had* any brains I would have,' he said with perfect indifference; nostalgia was no part of his make-up. 'Why, you sniffing around after something? There's a couple of 'orrible old things back there I need to clear out and have the room. Yeah, come round and have a look.'

I went into the back and Sid followed. There were two or three grimy motorheads back there in cut-offs over leather and black woolly-tops, working on a Harley Sportster, with a joint going round between them. On a bench at the back I spotted a CB radio.

'Deptford 'ells Angels,' Sid explained. 'These 'erbs are so poor they have to share a fag.' The bikers groaned at the old joke; they were long-hairs in flares so they were OK by me. Sid led me to a row of machines in the corner. I headed straight for a very tasty-looking Norton Dominator, a grey and chrome 88, but Sid explained that that was his.

The first thing we looked at was a late Triumph Daytona, a light, quick, city bike which should have been ideal, except that when you walked round the front the forks were bent back under the frame. I said no crash jobs; I didn't have the time or the money, and I wanted a runner. Next there was a plunger Flash, a 650 BSA twin; probably reliable, and nice-looking enough in its original paint, but a bit heavy for what I needed, a bit old and perhaps a bit too staid.

Sid pulled an old overcoat off the bike that was left. For a minute I thought it was a Fastback Commando, but that was just the shape of the one-piece seat-tank unit, a dark green Metisse fibre-glass affair. The bike was covered in mud and oil, with a big front wheel, knobbly tyres and a stubby, up-tilted silencer. I bent and looked at the tall engine, a big single-cylinder AMC job, a long-stroke 500 by the look it, with a mag at the front, an unusual looking one.

'A G80? Competition?' I said.

'That's right; Matchless rubbish. We turn north and curse Plumstead every time we try to get it going; the factory used to be just down the road. No, it's got a bit of history, that one. It was a scrambler, used to run on dope, like these 'erbs. Then the bloke who had it set it up for hill climbs; put in a compression plate, dropped it to nine and a half I think, and went back to petrol. The frame's off a Gold Star, with a lot of lugs chopped off.' (I winced internally – it seemed good BSA Gold Stars were fetching about two grand now and this guy had butchered one to make his special. Still, I thought, with this bike you might get the good handling without paying the price . . .) 'At the front it's got BSA yokes and Matchless forks. The rims are alloy, Borranis; he skimmed the fins off the front hub and drilled big holes in the rear one; all up it weighs about 340 pounds.'

'No good for the road though, I suppose?' I said casually.

'Yeah, he used to run it on the road,' said Sid, equally bored. 'Those tyres are Trials Universals, twenty-one-inch front, eighteen-inch rear, a bit dodgy in the wet but they'll do. There's a headlamp somewhere about; the ignition's off that Lucas Wader mag but I fixed him up with alternator electrics off the end of the crankshaft, and it worked all right.'

'Is he selling, then?' I said.

'He's not doing nothing,' Sid laughed. 'He was always a moody sod; lived with his mother, and they fought like cats and dogs. One day he was in 'ere, slamming about, so I tell him, Paul, either go out and ride your bike, or go 'ome and have a cup of tea. So he goes 'ome,' Sid concluded wearily, 'and smothers his mother, and now he's inside and asked me to get rid of this for him.'

'Pity,' I said, 'about the forks; they never made a decent front brake that would fit them. What year's the engine, anyway?'

'I think it's '59 or '60, something like that,' said Sid vaguely.

'Let's have a look. They put the year with the engine number,' I explained, leaning over the bike to look for the number at the base of the cylinder on the near side. And then stopped: there was just a blank space where it should have been stamped.

'It's registered though, I got the papers here,' Sid said quietly. 'You know I won't usually touch nothing dodgy, Jack; this one got landed on me.'

'Has it got an MOT?'

Sid gestured at a pad of blank MOT files on the counter and then, looking me guilelessly in the eyes, said, 'D'you think it'll pass?'

It was somehow already accepted that I was interested in relieving him of this dubiously legal crud-encrusted lump. There was no point at which I had made a conscious decision and now I tried to hedge, as much with myself as with him.

'I don't know if I'm interested in a competition bike on the road, really,' I said. 'They're always wrong, a lumpy engine and more power than you can ever use, you know?'

'It's funny you should say that,' said Sid, 'because that's one thing he always did say. You know hill climbs; private roads, people's long drives, lots of twists and turns, speed runs uphill against the clock. The bike with the most power should win but usually it doesn't work like that. You need something quick off the line, responsive, power of the right sort, know what I mean – usable. It's mostly in the ignition timing and the carb. People have started using speedway stuff, Jawa and JAP engines, but more than fifty horses and you've got to be really good to control it; you gear it down too low and it comes out of the corner on the rear wheel, front end pawing the air, death or glory stuff but you're losing seconds every time it happens.

'Now he always said this was just right; getting near ideal, like some of the scramblers now. He didn't muck about with it much; the G80 scrambler's valves were big already and the stock cam seemed right too. I saw him once or twice, he didn't do badly on everything but the longer hills; in the 500 class he had the legs off the other four-strokes, Velos and that, and most of the two-strokes too. But suit yourself.'

'It's probably clapped, bored out to the limit,' I said defensively.

'He rebuilt that engine last year, first time, and all it needed was a plus 20 piston,' said Sid. I'd have to trust him on that. I was walking round it now, looking for objections.

'The big carb,' I said. 'Too fierce. No way you can get the bits.'

'It's a funny thing,' said Sid mildly, 'that's what he found. He wanted an Amal GP but he couldn't get one, so he put on a Monobloc, a plain 390, while he was looking, and it worked so well he kept it. See? And I bodged him that box air filter after it started misfiring at high revs, running over-rich.'

'I'd have to hear it,' I said hopelessly.

'Help yourself,' said Sid, gesturing at the tools all around and wandering off to serve a customer.

Within ten minutes I'd involved the 'erbs – I hadn't been able to remember which way was advance on the advance/retard lever on the high, cross-braced handlebars. Kicking the engine over produced a big fat nothing, though compression was good enough to make you sweat. I did everything I should have with the petrol lines and the electrics for half an hour, and then one of them went out for tea, and we sat around talking about their CB rig and saying 'pository' for yes and such. I got back to it and after an hour the bike was still an infuriatingly inert lump of metal. Sid was pissing himself and I was nearly ready to cry, but rather than pack it in I started all over again.

We had changed the hard plug, so now I took out the new N5 and checked it; then I noticed that the gap was closed right up. The old plug had been dirty and the new one had a fraction

25

too long a reach so it was knocking the piston and closing up. Unwilling to believe that it was as simple as that, I waited while Sid found a new FE 220; then tightened it down, snapped on the h.t. lead, checked the air lever was closed, turned on the petrol, tickled the carb, set the lever just back from full advance, used the decompressor to ease the piston over the top with the kick-start, found compression again and, realizing by this time why they had invented electric starters, I held the throttle very nearly closed and taking a deep breath gave it a long, hard kick.

There was a deafening flat bang and I looked down to see smoke rising from the air filter. The lads applauded the backfire, and nervously I tried again.

It caught. It was like being in a Bofors gun position: deafening concussions, slow at first, rocked the enclosed space as a cloud of oily smoke began to puff back out from the silencer, the oil that had accumulated in the crankcase burning off and the sweet sharp smell of vegetable-based Castrol R filling the air. Sid and the long-hairs were choking and cheering. I concentrated on nursing the engine, feeding it a little more throttle, easing the air lever open after a while, listening hard for nasty noises in the first important moments. There was nothing I could detect and once I got used to the noise I realized it was actually a pleasant exhaust note, the concussions sharp and staccato but not harsh.

After that, of course, I had to take it out. There was a tax disc by the front wheel, but when you looked closely the thing behind the glass was a folded Guinness label. I had a licence but no insurance for a bike, but Sid wasn't bothered. We checked the petrol and wheeled the spluttering thumper out into the summer afternoon. Outside, the up-tilted front end, kicked-up silencer and the great tower of the engine could be seen to better advantage; it was a ready-looking machine and I felt a large twinge of apprehension. One of the 'erbs kept it going until I had put on my sunglasses and Sid's silver pudding-basin helmet and got a leg over. I pulled in the clutch and clonked awkwardly into first, just caught it as it tried to stall, and after a minute began easing out the clutch until that moment when I felt it start to bite and the concussions began to impel me forward and away down the road.

For five minutes I eased gingerly around the back streets, getting the feel of it, going very easy on the throttle; finding the back brake seemed fine, the front a bit spongy, and handling good as far as I tried it, which was not very far. And sure enough, like the man had said, the motor was very responsive, though, at the low speeds I was doing, every one of its concussions seemed to jar straight up my backbone. It was fine as far as it went but, when I reached the High Street, on impulse I didn't turn back towards Sid's but hung a right, towards Shooter's Hill.

Five minutes trickling past the plastic shop-fronts of the High Street gave me plenty of time to think about what would happen if the law pulled me (though I had noticed that in town at any rate they seemed to have too much on their plates to worry about traffic nuisances) or if the bike stalled and I had to try and get it started again. But it did seem to handle the heavy traffic well, ticking over steadily, pulling away from a halt easily, the back brake at least stopping it dead with no fuss, and the exhaust note turning some heads but not producing scowls, just interested looks. To have to keep damping back the power just as it began to develop was annoying; but, as it was, the bike would do in town.

Then I had cleared the traffic and reached the bottom of the long hill. This was it and, gathering self and machine, at about forty in top I twisted the throttle two-thirds open. The bike flew forward. Very quickly I was pulling it round some cars in front, leaving them standing, feeling a fine breathless lift as the roaring motor's mightly torque shoved us effortlessly up the hill; as the gradient steepened I thought about changing down, but instead tried more throttle and we leapt forward faster still, the motor had apparently endless bottom, and burst over the crest of the hill to shoot down the far side; where, a mile further on at the lights at the bottom, the front brake gave me a few heart-stopping moments before bringing us to a halt.

A slow mile later and I came up to the big roundabout at the top of the long hill which lead down to the river and the Blackwall Tunnel. There was traffic coming in from there on the right and for the first time I pulled away from a standstill quickly, slipping into the stream effortlessly and giving no offence because the power delivery was so precise; you thought where you wanted to go and you were there. I took the roundabout fast, heeled over all the way; I'm not a scratcher, but the plain metal footrests scraped on the way round, they had grounded before I had realized it – the thing seemed to steer itself and encourage you to go the limit, even on those tyres. Three-quarters of the way round I switched in a long S-turn from hard right lean to hard left and swung down into the approach road beside the underpass, changed up into third and rode straight out on to the three-lane dual carriage-way and down towards the tunnel.

I pulled out fast across all three lanes, changing up and passing a couple of lorries and some cars ahead, and screwed it on. The feel and the noise of the motor's individual concussions had blended into one rising flat roar now. My jacket was ballooning in the wind, I could feel the straps of Sid's helmet pulling under my chin as it was tugged backwards, and tears from the wind were streaming out beside my shades, the industrial waste land opening out beside the descending road just a blurred tunnel as I hurled down the winding, undulating grey-brown tarmac, the needle on the speedo flickering midway between seventy and eighty with what felt like plenty more in hand. A Cortina was hogging the fast lane; I pulled by on the inside and snapping a glance back to see him seem to be accelerating, found more speed effortlessly and rode a ribbon of it down to the last exit before the tunnel, where, braking, I slid over to the left, changed down and pulled off down the ramp for Greenwich; then, crossing beneath the underpass in second, catching the sweet yeasty smell of the brewery nearby,

I revved up two or three times and pulled back on to the dual carriageway again to repeat the performance in the other direction.

I got back to Sid's a quarter of an hour later, pulled in outside the garage and, after a moment's looking around for a non-existent ignition switch, killed the motor with the advance/retard and sat with my ears ringing, digesting the ride. After a couple of minutes Sid wandered out and said, 'Thought you'd dropped it.'

I took a deep breath and said, 'Nah, but I might have. I told you that front brake wasn't too clever.'

Sid just looked at me, and after a while I gave up and said, 'All right, how much?'

There was a bit of horse-trading; he knew I wanted it but I knew he might have a job shifting it with the engine number gone, and a street scrambler special wasn't to most people's taste anyway. We waltzed around for a bit but in the end he did right by me and I left with change from £350. He said he'd find the lights and fit them; I tried to get him to throw in new road tyres and a quart of Castrol R but he wouldn't budge, so I paid him there and then for the oil, plus VAT; I still didn't understand VAT but when I asked Sid about it all he had to offer was, 'I dunno who he is, but he must be making a lot of money.'

I handed over my savings and we arranged for him to do the tyres and an MOT, and I'd come for it when I had the money to pay for them. Sid's last remark was, 'Going to join the Owner's Club?' and when I said I'd think about it, 'Smoke a pipe, do you? You'll need to.'

I shouted, 'Ten-Ten,' the truckers' goodbye, to the Deptford Angels and left, carrying my oil can, a bit apprehensive but deep down well pleased. After that I tried to get Blithers to fit the van out with a CB rig, but he wasn't having any, so I had to be content with trucker talk on the phone to Deborah from then on.

I picked up the bike a week later, and by the end of the summer there'd been some changes made, but mostly superficial ones. I traded the big front wheel for a nineteen-inch road one with a larger but still imperfect front brake, and fitted narrower straight handlebars and a bar-end mirror. I soon stopped using Castrol R, not having either the money to afford it or the patience for the long warm-up period. Though it wasn't really built for it I wanted to be able to take birds on the pillion, so I swopped the single-seat Metisse unit with Sid who dug up a second-hand BSA dual seat and a two-gallon steel export tank; then I threw the low profile that sense dictated to the winds and had the tank sprayed bright Matchless red, with a single silver pin-stripe around the panels and a big silver M-for-Matchless transfer – the frame may have been BSA but the heart and soul of the bike was that tall one-lung motor.

I kept the bike in the square, slipped in between the rusting hulks near our front door and chained up tight under a grimy cover, and just had to hope it would escape the attentions of both Ranking Peanut and our neighbour's boy Derek and his hammer. Working on it out in the street could be good sometimes, with the punk's girlfriend, a lithe, blazing-haired roller-disco queen, doing her stuff on her own wheels, turning spectacular cartwheels or giving the kids rides on her shoulders while people stopped to chat with me about the bike. It never needed a lot of attention; as Sid had suggested, I kept the carb clean and a regular eye on the points, and there were never any problems, except starting it sometimes which could have you sweating and cursing.

But all that was forgotten on the move. All that summer and autumn, some evenings and most weekends I would be out, riding carefully in the traffic for the early city miles, out north along Black Horse Road or south to the tunnel, until I reached Epping Forest or the hill outside Sevenoaks and could let it out a bit. I always loved that moment of transformation when you cranked it on, the power bit and rose, and the thing was changed from a plodding thumper to Supermatchless, a roaring red streak of power. I rarely exceeded eighty, I was sometimes passed by grinning, whizzing factions of The Youth; but when I felt like it and everything was right, at traffic lights and in the winding lanes and A-roads, I would let the G80's hill-geared torque and handling do its stuff, and blow selected Jap crap into the weeds.

Chapter 3

I learned to value both the bike and the van during the next lonely months, as the winter drew in and most evenings would find me wearily climbing the stairs to the attic, clutching a bag of Chinese food, rain spattering on the low windows in the dark outside, after a day spent driving past the stages of my age and youth.

As I have mentioned, the past was much on my mind, and I kept thinking I saw people I had known. Not five minutes from the square I would cruise past a ground-floor window where my first serious lady, Sheila, had lived, and where we had pursued our stormy way together until one drunken evening I'd put my fist through all six panes of that front window and walked out of her life for good. I knew Sheila did not live there any more, but she was probably still in London. It was a tantalizing situation in many ways, being on the scene of most of my past – the places where I had first made friends, known girls, chemical ecstasies and adventures; but unable now to speak to the figures who had acted in that past with me.

So I would pass most of my evenings in the attic. I fooled around with the painting a bit; I was going to an evening class once a week. I never did get a telly, but I listened to the few records I had bought on a second-hand stereo Deborah had lent me; or, on a tiny transistor called the Citizen Mod, heard the news of mounting unemployment and the Irish bombs beginning to go off around the city. I also read a lot, as I had done in Argentina, often with great pleasure; the opening of *David Copperfield*, 'whether I shall turn out to be the hero of my own life', struck a big chord, and often this book or that would excite me by seeming to offer an answer, a system I could live by. But I could never keep it up long enough to make the necessary connections; always, somehow, the energy seeped away and finally I would be too low to read even Raymond Chandler or a bike magazine. Then sometimes, especially if the traffic had been bad or I had come up against some snotty receptionist or client during a pick-up that day, I would ask myself in despair whether this was how I was going to end up, a mild grotesque, a van driver on my own in a single room. Or I'd be really brought down at being broke all the time, and start angrily scheming one more quick deal to get me clear. Or then again tremble with dread at the thought of the past, in the shape of vengeful hoods, catching up with me.

But I learned that these moods never lasted long, and that afterwards I would be left once more up against the problem: my memories, and my inability to make sense of them. I didn't spend the whole time agonizing, you understand, but mostly just wondering what had happened and what it meant. Then I would light a candle and, lying down on the bed, stare at the four or five photographs and postcards I had tacked to the wooden shelf above. There was one of my old girlfriend Sheila, a portrait that Freddy had taken; I had burned the original glossy blow-up he had given me, but he had been able to find the negative and do another smaller print. There was a postcard of a village in the Dordogne; a scuffed black and white picture of the corrals and buildings and poplar trees of the *estancia* in Argentina; and a colour picture of two figures leaning on motorbikes and squinting into the sun outside the granite steps of a stone-built barn in Cornwall. That was me and my mate Denny, over ten years ago in the summer of 1970.

So that was why I valued the wheels so much; I had learned that you could cruise in a car or on a bike, drift over vortices and fire-pits, warps and yawps of time and feelings that otherwise could take you right down, swallow you altogether. For sometimes my whole life seemed to be contracting down to that one room; the spaghetti of tangled wires behind the record player, the spiral whorls of dust on the rug, my memories and my inability to understand them. For my memories, and especially the images of those pictures, insinuated themselves as part of a subterranean pattern of coincidence, of connection in my life which, again and again, I always seemed to be one step away from interpreting. And whose inevitable companion was the plunge into nightmare.

For the rest, I was like anyone else would be in that situation: I didn't sleep well, went to work like a zombie, drank too much and was possessed by a sad-eyed and mostly ineffectual lust, still looking fitfully for salvation to come from a girl.

I eventually pulled one of the women from the painting class: a mouse, but with a trim figure and a pert face, and I can't pretend that I was that detached or picky. She seemed nervous when we got to the room but, after a couple of glasses of wine, went to the bathroom and came out naked. After we'd done it, which my own nerves made a brief business, she told me for the first time that she was married, that her husband said she was frigid, and that the reason she had decided to bunk up with me was, get this, she had read an article in a magazine entitled nothing less than 'How Adultery Can Save Your Marriage'. Very twentieth century. After a second marginally more successful go-round I was able to reassure her on the subject of frigidity, and she left quite pleased; but the cumulative bleakness of the encounter had me sitting on the bed hugging myself and rocking, holding my guts and moaning; the full bedsit syndrome. Whether due to a saved marriage or a fat lip from her husband, she never came to class again, so that was that. I was left with nothing sexier than the smell of bacon, and a night out was once again a walk to the launderette and then coming home to play pelmanism with my socks.

I definitely needed cheering up, which is why when Andy, one of the long-distance drivers at work, mentioned that he'd had a little power-assistance on his last run, I said, ' "Poppin' little white pills and my eyes are open wide"?' and, when he nodded, let him know I was well interested; speed has always been kind to me and I felt I could use some now. So three days later I arranged to see him in a pub just south of London Bridge, a small grubby house squeezed under the railway arches by Borough Market beside Southwark Cathedral, where Andy met his man.

I got there early and, easing the bike into the shadows below the railway bridge, sat on it checking out the pub as the trains rattled and thundered overhead. Though it was well off what had been my patch, I wasn't eager to have the dealer turn out to be someone I had known. But no one I recognized went in, so I peered through a window and saw the driver sitting with a young skinheaded geezer whom Andy introduced to me as Doctor Lockyer; when I asked why they just told me to look in the cathedral. What the Doctor had that day was sulphate, powder. Andy took twenty quid's worth but for openers I only went in for five; powder is too easy to cut. The Doctor laughed and said that I didn't just look a gift horse in the mouth, I wanted to take its bleeding temperature as well. He left, and Andy took me into the cathedral and pointed out the tomb which held the original Doctor Lockyer, with the epitaph as follows:

His virtues and his PILLS are so well known,
That envy can't confine them under stone

The current Doctor had evidently more wit than his bog-brush haircut suggested. I said goodbye to Andy and got the Matchless out from in front of a row of derelict houses rotting under the railway bridge like a Dickensian stage set. I just squeezed the bike through a narrow set of bollards out on to the pavement on the west side of London Bridge and rode away over it, wondering, as I always did crossing the bridges, at the shining view of the city; and went home.

There I decanted the sulphate into Coldrex capsules, and tried one for work the next day. It turned out to be fizzing stuff and I skated around my circuit that day with my hands tight on the wheel, my eyes jammed open and a maniac grin

35

on my lips; and when I knocked off, poured down a couple of pints of lager in the pub with Deborah and kissed her for the first time – it started as a half-joking kiss of goodbye, but she closed her eyes and opened her wide mouth and did some amazing things with her tongue. This cheered me up no end temporarily, and naturally from then on I attempted to pursue the matter with her from time to time; but Deborah was sweetly evasive, evidently still heavily into her geezer in Stockwell. Though it did spice up going to work for a while.

But at bottom I still didn't know what to do with myself. I reckoned I could make it but sometimes, with Christmas approaching, the feelings of despair were quite overwhelming. One lonely eveing I came home from work with my nerves banging and twitching and decided to run a bath; I turned on the water and then went into my room and put on a Dire Straits record, them being one of the few positive things that had happened to music while I had been away as far as I could see. After a while I went in to check the bath water. There seemed to be a lot of shit in it that I hadn't noticed before. Then, looking again, I realized there was a great gaping hole in the wall above; the thick plaster grille which let in air had fallen off the wall into the bath and was lying, surrounded by cement rubble, at the bottom of the clear water.

Things were falling apart, it seemed, and I didn't know whether to laugh or cry. I left the bath, got dressed and walked to the phone in the launderette. There were five S. Rayners in the phone book but I got lucky on the third one, and after all those years found myself talking to Sheila again.

Chapter 4

Because when I returned and returned to the past, Sheila, above all, was what it was about.

What do you say, *hypocrite lecteur*, when you're talking about someone who was so much a part of your life that for a time the two seemed to be the same: 'my first girlfriend', 'the girl I was serious about', or just 'a girl I used to know'? What *do* you say, *semblable, mon frère*?

I've said all those things about Sheila. She was a short, fair-haired girl with a firm generous body; her hair, her skin, all of her seemed silky, somehow, glistening. She had been studying art at the Royal College when I first knew her, and had an art student's understated dress sense, and reticence, and application. She played the guitar, too; one of the things I would remember when sitting in the attic was a night at her home in Surrey; her widowed father away for the weekend, just the two of us, her sitting cross-legged in a short skirt in front of the fire, bent over the shiny pale torso of her guitar, silky blonde hair falling over her face, playing the deep chords of 'All My Trials'; and me knowing I *would* remember it all my life, whenever I smelt wood-smoke or heard the tune.

Oh yes. But how do you reconcile the need to go your own ways with the need, the apparently insatiable need, for each other, which no one else came close to satisfying? For we were going in different directions. I was drifting into bikes and dealing; she, despite or because of the Surrey background, was a Young Socialist, had a social conscience and when she left college as well as making jewellery had got into part-time adult education, teaching at Tower Hamlets. Each of us seemed to threaten the other.

After so many false endings and helpless reconciliations, such jealousy, so many quarrels – I would even find myself getting at her about her retired Royal Navy father, her only surviving relative of whom she was very fond – so much grinding unpleasantness and pain, the final window-smashing break when it came left more relief than regret, because our dues were paid in full. I was getting ready to set up the drug scam that was to be the source of all my troubles, and after that I was off and running until the present time. Back in London, at first I had not felt the old compulsion to look her up, and when I did remember it all in Barnsbury the thoughts curled around my room as lazily and aimlessly as smoke; though sometimes I thought there would never be any breasts as fine for me, such hair, such silky skin.

There was a blunt Argentine proverb on the subject of lovers' reconciliations: never light the same cigarette twice. But now it was not her body I longed for but her friendship. She had always had an old-fashioned way about her; she considered things – after you had said something, sometimes she would pause while she looked at you, not so much a scrutiny as careful listening – sometimes, especially when I hadn't been sure of myself, the habit would enrage me. Old-fashioned, too, was her precise enunciation when she spoke, and her low, rather musical voice. I wanted all that now. I suppose I really wanted her to tell me who I was, what to do.

On the phone she sounded very surprised, and pleased to hear me, but then one of the old pauses came and I guessed she was remembering all the trouble between us. We arranged to meet for a drink at lunchtime on neutral territory, a pub we used to go to near London University.

It was a bright, blowy morning; we arrived at the same time, and the first sight I caught of her was on the other side of the road, walking up Malet Street, silhouetted against the gleaming wall of the Union building. It sounds stupid, but have you ever noticed how good a woman looks who walks with her legs slightly bent? I had forgotten that, and the set of her shoulders that held her breasts so proud; the wind in the street was blowing back her tan quilted waistcoat and flattening her blouse and skirt against her body. I had seen her first and gazed

38

for a long moment, realizing why I had not got in touch before. Then she spotted me and crossed the road, and I went to meet her. We didn't touch or embrace, but looked at each other's faces. There were smile-lines, and a hint of weariness around her grey-blue eyes, but no more than that. I doubted if I had worn as well, what with booze, drugs and three years' beating from the Argentine weather.

Then she smiled – her mouth was wide, her eyes could stay sad but sort of amused with their own sadness, as before – and broke the silence, her low voice almost a murmur.

'Hello, Jack. You should have said about the beard.'

I smiled ruefully.

'Hello, Sheila. Long time no see.'

But it was all right. From the start something told me there was no chance, and no point, to our taking up where we had left off, even though I soon discovered she had never married, and was now living alone in the East End in her own house by the river, on the Isle of Dogs. But also right that from that first meeting we found a great rapport existed between us; maybe more than before, now that the physical attraction was kept banked down. In the past we had known each other really well and, allowing for the passing of time (which initially I was not prepared to do), we still did. I could finally talk to someone about my distress both at, without going into too much detail, the way my own life had been, and absurd though it sounds, at the way the things we had all believed when we were together were now apparently being eroded and defeated at every turn.

Ironically, it was talking about the old days that clinched the platonic nature of our scene. Sheila had known few of the faces I hung out with then, but we did have one friend in common: my principal wild-man mate from those days, Denny Lee. They had met through me and, like her, Denny had been actively into radical politics. We had all gone on the big demonstrations against the war in Vietnam which had ended up outside the American Embassy in Grosvenor Square, and I

39

remember after the horses had charged and the police gone in swinging, watching in horror as the two of them tried to overturn a car to block the road round the square. I had dragged them away from it before they succeeded, being convinced that it just wasn't that sort of street fighting yet. So naturally I asked if she had seen Denny any more.

There was one of her long listening silences, and then she raised her grey-blue eyes to look at me and said, 'Yes; from time to time. We're together, Jack.'

I felt a pang of something, I didn't know what. I said, 'Is he around? Can we meet?'

She shook her head.

'He's away south, travelling,' and when I went to ask her where she just said, 'you know, *travelling*; you should know, you used to do it too.'

I nodded slowly, taking this in. Because Denny and I had run a couple of numbers together, when I had been dealing; and she seemed to be saying that he was still in the life. I had guessed he might be, which is why I had not tried to get in touch with him before; and couldn't really afford to now. So all I said was, 'What about Alice?'

'She's back living in Cornwall, down at Trecarrick. They split up three years ago. She had his baby, a little girl; but if you didn't know, don't tell anyone. Everyone down there thinks it was somebody else's.'

I had not known. Denny and Alice had been a fixture when we had all been together. Alice was a magnificent black-haired Cornish lady who came from a large farming family from outside St Ives; we had all gone down to their farm on bikes for her sister's wedding once, and that was where the picture of me and Denny was taken which I still had by my bed. I was sorry but not surprised that the two of them had split up; nothing lasts forever, and that had gone double with Denny. But, despite his being with Sheila now and despite the other reason not to do it, I was looking forward to running into him again.

40

Just being with Sheila took me out of myself. We started meeting for lunch or a drink and then, tentatively at first, the films or a theatre, even a gallery once or twice; suddenly the town seemed to have a bit more to offer. Without actually saying much, she showed me rather than told me that things might not be as bad as I had gloomily decided, and that there were still people trying to do something about the all-encroaching shit. I went to a party or two and met some of her liberal-left friends, teachers, journalists and so on, and after initial mistrust I even began to like and half respect some of them. (Deborah at work noticed that I'd perked up a bit and asked me cheekily if some pavement princess had taken pity on me. I told her a big negatory to that, and when was she coming through?)

So when Christmas Day rolled around, and I had got clear of the hectic West End traffic and the drunks bellowing obscenely at the van in Fleet Street or slurred and frantically merry in the offices where I called, Sheila asked me and some other friends over to her place. Her father was too ill to leave the old people's home where, after being involved in a bad car smash, he now spent his time in a wheelchair – there was a sad hint of reduced circumstances about that, after their place in Surrey – so both Sheila and I were alone that Christmas.

I had never visited her house before. Christmas morning I slept late and, when I woke, lay in bed for a while thinking about other Christmases. When I got up it was a cold day, windy but dry. I made tea, got dressed and then fired up the Matchless and headed down the quiet roads towards Bethnal Green and south from there, then swung left into East India Dock Road, riding through streets deserted except for hurrying families of brightly swathed Pakistanis, until I reached an old church and a Bingo hall Sheila had told me to look out for, where I turned right for Millwall and the east side of the Isle of Dogs. I swung down a road lined with a corrugated-iron fence on one side with the Thames out of sight behind it, and on the other a dark brick wall crowding in concealing the docks of the Blackwall Basin, with only the occasional crane poking up above it to give you a clue. I clattered over a narrow, fixed iron bridge, and soon after crossed a wider more modern one, painted turquoise and liable to be raised when ships emerged down a channel from the basin on the right out into the river. In the wide tree-lined road, unexpected in the docks, immediately after the bridge, I spotted a row of houses on the right and pulled over to a halt. Sheila had said hers was the end one nearest the bridge. I parked the bike, took off my helmet, unstrapped a flat parcel from the back of the pillion and knocked on the door; while I waited, a boisterous shaggy black mongrel gave me his best attention. Then the door opened and Sheila stood there in a stunning cerise party dress, her hair up.

'Leave him alone, Tramp,' she said to the dog, who trotted off happily. We exchanged kisses on the cheek and she said, 'God, Jack, your face is freezing. Come up.'

We clattered up the stripped and varnished stairs, past a door on the second landing half-open to reveal a white-carpeted bedroom, with, six feet off the floor, a big bunk bed up on a platform; and up on to a half-landing which led out through two glass-panelled french doors to the back of the house and a clear view out over the docks, cranes and empty waterways of the Blackwall Basin. A clear view because Sheila had put double-glazed glass panels from floor to sloping ceiling where the outside wall had been and turned the place into an indoor greenhouse, with tropical plants and ferns everywhere in the humid warmth from a permanent gas heating system, and fronds curling around the wrought-iron pillars. In a section separated by fine wire mesh, two scarlet parakeets and many small bright-coloured birds whirled and fluttered, disturbed by our intrusion.

I nodded approval and said, 'Me Tarzan? But I wouldn't like to have your heating bills. And what do the neighbours make of it?'

'All the kids love it,' she said. 'Now come up and meet the others.'

The top floor was all one room, and again tall glass windows at the back and front gave grand views back over the Docks and out over the river, winding up from Greenwich and round Blackwall, over the tunnel I had ridden down to from Sid's, and through the industrial landscape, the gas works, power station and the pungent brewery, on its way to Tilbury and the sea.

There were some people standing by the back window, and I put down my helmet and the parcel I was carrying for Sheila, and went over to be introduced. The last guy I shook hands with, a big bloke named Frank, in a smart-looking light-coloured soft leather jacket, nodded at the helmet and said, with a trace of accent, Scots or Irish, 'A hard man, braving the elements today. What kind of bike have you got?'

I started to tell him about the Matchless when Sheila cut us off with, 'For God's sake, Frank, don't start him talking bikes, not yet anyway.'

'All right, Mrs,' I said, 'and speaking of that I'd better give you your present.'

I handed her the package and, as she removed the paper, experienced some misgivings; I hadn't really meant her to open it in front of other people. It was a painting I had done and got framed, the one from the photograph of me and Denny on our bikes outside the barn at Trecarrick; just a water-colour because I had done it at home, but I was quite pleased with the way the colours had come out, the granite and pasture in sunlight, though possibly it was overbalanced in favour of the totemic machines, the bikes. Denny stared out, fair-haired, with a lazy grin, while I had been looking across at him.

Sheila held it at arm's length, then kissed my cheek and said, 'My two main men. It's good, Jack; it brings it all back.'

'Is that not Dennis?' said a voice and I turned to see the big bloke, Frank, looking over our shoulders.

'Yeah, do you know him?' I asked.

'Yes,' said Frank, squinting at the picture, 'but I think not for as long as you have. It's good.'

'I met Frank through Denny,' said Sheila, taking our arms and leading us to meet the others.

We were six. There was Stephen, a friend of hers I had met before, a middle-aged guy who ran a jewellery shop and workshop in Covent Garden where Sheila did her stuff a couple of days a week. He was currently rather down as his arm was in plaster after a late and ill-conceived attempt to get into roller-disco; his large and ebullient red-haired wife, an infant-school teacher who was there with him, had probably egged him on to it.

And there was Frank, Frank McMillen, a guy about my age but three inches taller and built on the generous scale, with receding fair hair and silver-rimmed glasses that changed their tint with the light. At first, as I've said, I couldn't tell from his accent whether he was Scots or Irish (it was the latter) and I thought he was running a bit flash, with the glasses, and loafers with tassels, and the fawn-coloured soft leather hip-length blouson jacket, every inch the off-duty businessman, which is what he was. But he liked bikes; and I liked his Swedish girl-friend, a full-bodied blonde called Tusi with little English language but no Scandinavian melancholy at all; and I certainly enjoyed the crate of good champagne he had provided for the party. Clearly he was into wine for he had also bought Sheila a crate of claret as a present; but that was stashed under the side-board nailed shut, and he forbade her to touch or move it for another couple of years. By the time we were halfway through the champagne, and we'd all lost to him at an uproarious game of Cluedo, I had decided ol' Frank was OK by me, and that I'd hold the Irish jokes to a minimum.

We drank Buck's Fizz until it was time for the meal; they were all there for it, on the basis that Stephen with his arm couldn't cook and his wife didn't, though she had brought the Christmas pudding; Tusi would have been wasted at it and Frank couldn't be bothered – he was off the next day, leaving his rented apartment and commuting to Saudi where he ran a contract labour set-up; and I of course was stuck because there's no such thing as a Chinese Christmas dinner. So we all sat down around a plain hexagonal table in the circle of light under a blue and turquoise art-nouveau leaded lampshade, and fell to on Sheila's turkey stuffed with oysters ('Ah, the succulent bi-valves,' Frank observed) and all the trimmings. Our waistlines expanded, the pudding flamed and Stephen pronounced the brandy butter to be 'better than an orgasm', a statement his wife qualified with 'better than one of yours, anyhow', at which Tusi, in a rare moment of comprehension, laughed so hard she nearly fell off her chair.

After that we sat around drinking brandy, eating satsumas and cracking nuts in the mouth of an iron dog constructed for that purpose whose jaws were operated by depressing its tail. While his wife helped Sheila to clear up, Stephen rolled joints one-handed. As the dark fell over the docks outside the tall windows, I was able to tell Frank all about the Matchless; it turned out he had yearned for a British bike as he'd had great times in his youth on an ancient but faithful BSA twin.

'An A10?' I asked.

'That's right – the Golden Flash,' Frank said, relishing the words.

'I don't know if you're interested,' I said, 'but I might know where you could come by one of them, if you still wanted. But it's 1953, a plunger job.'

'That was the very year I had!' he exclaimed, draining his brandy glass. 'But I suppose it's been messed about with?'

'No, it's OK; the original paint and everything, as far as I could see.'

'Perfect,' said Frank. 'Who has it? Is it a shop? How do I get in touch?'

At this point there was a pause as Stephen handed me a joint; and I must admit that I then indulged in a little mild prevarication. As middleman in this deal with the patently affluent Frank, I could see getting a fair price for Sid (for it was his bike I had in mind), and still doing myself a bit of good. But not if I put Frank in touch with Sid direct. So I just said, 'No, it's a bit tricky; it's an old guy I know and he could pull a moody about letting it go; I think I can get him to sell, but leave it to me to begin with. Where can I get in touch with you, when you're back?'

Frank had the joint. He took a hit, looked thoughtful for a moment, but then pulled out a tiny leather-bound memo pad from an inside pocket and scribbled a number on it.

'If the feller wants to sell, ask for me there in a couple of months. And thanks for your trouble. Now tell me, Jack, about you and Denny in the old days. He's a terrible man still, so God knows how he was then.'

I looked at him for a while.

'You know it's funny, but it's hard,' I said after a bit, feeling the good grass and drink slowing me down, having to take care not to sentimentalize. 'When you're that close to someone it can be hard to see them clearly. Back in the sixties it was like he was part of me; maybe that's why I'd so like to get in touch with him again, it would be sort of like getting in touch with a part of myself . . . I don't know. In real terms – he was always brighter than me, and it seemed, sometimes, he had no fear at all. Crazy of course; *further out* was his word.

'I remember one time, we'd been in a club up West and Denny was with this girl he was after, Stephanie, quite a posh tart, divorced, who up till then hadn't wanted to know. But that night they went well over the top; we did a bottle of tequila and half a gramme of coke in the club – Denny had just got back from Peru – and then took off back to Stephanie's place, her leading the way in her Mini Cooper and the two of us trying to keep up in Denny's old Anglia. The trouble was she was totally out of it; she started racing, it was a bit foggy but we were doing eighty down the Mall, and then I spotted a wrong-looking car, you know, two big blokes and a complicated aerial. So Denny flashes her to slow down but there's nothing doing, she mounts the kerb going round the monument at Buck House, and ends up at the lights in

46

Buckingham Gate next to these geezers, who by now are giving her the hard eye.

'She'll wise up now, says Denny, but not a bit of it. When the lights changed she dumped cork and raced them away; they chase her and she turns hard right across them, a narrow miss it was, we were covering our eyes, and then she shoots up a one-way street the wrong way; Denny follows, passes the fuzz and then totally insanely tries to block them out, he's weaving left and right and they're flashing and honking, and finally they pass him and catch Stephanie.

'Denny drives on about a quarter of a mile, then stops the car and we stagger back and find the two of them hulking over her; they've had a fright, see, and they're well peeved. And let alone the nonsense in the motors, Denny's having trouble standing, it takes immense concentration for him to articulate but again, insanity, he takes one of them by the coat sleeve, *confidentially*, he's winking, whispering; he draws this guy aside and keeping his head carefully down explains that Steph is under "immense emotional strain" – as they've just broken off their engagement!

'The cop was staring at him incredulously and then Stephanie, who's heard, cracks up completely; she's pissing herself, she's laughing so hard she nearly falls out of the car. The cop says, look at her: she was doing eighty *in the fog*, she was racing us, she went the wrong way up a one-way street and not one but *two* tests show she's about ten times over the limit; emotional strain *no way*, they're taking her to the station. But by a miracle they leave us out of it. Back at the car Denny's too drunk to find out where the station is in the *A to Z*. I have to do it. And when we get there she'd been moved to another one. That's when I got a taxi home. But next time I see him he tells me they didn't release her till five in the morning. He takes her home and, typically, that's the moment she decides they should make it. But – there's a visitor in her proper bed, so they have to bundle in with her five-year-old son; and when Denny's finally at it, the kid wakes up —'

'Oh Lord,' said Frank.

'That's what I thought, not too clever, but Denny said it didn't faze the kid at all. He knew Denny, and he simply climbed on top of his back and started bouncing up and down on top of the pair of them; he thought it was the most sensible thing Stephanie had done in ages, having a good bounce on the bed...'

Sheila came out of the kitchen in time to hear the end of it and said apologetically to Frank, 'Jack's not boring you with the old days again, is he?'

'No, just a little tale about our friend Denny; I never knew he had all that anarchy in him.'

'Oh no,' I cut in, 'if anarchy is a mind without a system, Denny wasn't that: he always had a system, and he could make you believe in it too. It was just that he used to keep changing them.'

'That's true, he could do that,' said Sheila. 'Now Jack would be the anarchist, if he stayed in one place long enough to be anything. But he's a romantic really; in those days he had his ecstasy, now he has his melancholy —'

'What is this?' I protested. 'Get the Guest? What I am is just an ageing rocker, and if I don't much like the way things are going, can you wonder? All around, day after day, you see the hopelessness; the offices I go to are overheated and dead, the streets grimy and indifferent, the newspapers and radio chattering fatuous, like housewives holding back the suburban panics; and the countryside, from what I've seen, more and more of it looks like the views you only used to catch from train windows coming into the city, riding the rails up the arsehole of industrial society, but the muck is spreading now.

'And what have you got to put up against all this? An index-linked pension; or where we sang the body electric, now you've got the freaking punks, and madness. Which doesn't look too clever to me; I reckon a counter-culture should *be* a culture, something to sustain freaks and rejects and help them find what's best in themselves. All this lot seems to offer is the

48

wrong kind of madness, and despair and, even if it's only a pose, that's not too nourishing.'

'Maybe it's the most relevant counsel just now,' said Frank.

'If that's so, you can expect the bombs to go on going off here like they do where you come from,' I said, and realized as I did so that my unexpected talent for polemic had brought conversation to a halt.

Sheila said, 'You still haven't learned, Jack. You pay for history; the years, centuries of injustice go in the blood. And then you pay ...'

'As Denny always used to say,' I came back, and her shrug admitted that she was repeating him – just as I had used to do; it was hard not to because he put things so well and memorably.

Frank just smiled and said, 'I know what you mean but I can't agree with either of you. Over there it's like over here; just a few hot-heads who get a lot of publicity, and the rest of us wanting to get on with our lawful occasions. Besides, Jack, aren't you overdoing the glory of the sixties a wee bit? I've had better times at sing-songs with the guys in a hut in Saudi than I ever did at most pop concerts ...'

'Ah, but were you at Monterey?' I started to ask, when Sheila said softly but with an edge, 'No – that was a fine speech you made, Jack. But what are you going to do about it all?'

'What can you do?' I shrugged. 'Just try and stay loose.' This was getting just like old times; Sheila and I were squaring off to one another when Frank smiled again and said, 'Yes, Jack's the anarchist, and I'll drink to that. Here's long life and liberty to us all. Sheila, my love, will you not get down that instrument and give us a tune?'

After some persuading Sheila got up and unhooked her guitar from the wall. The moment had passed, and I was relieved; all I seemed capable of was flailing away verbally, and if I felt that Frank had glossed things over, well, as Denny had also used to say, people mostly don't think, they just repeat slogans to themselves.

Soon I was lost in the pleasure of hearing Sheila play again;

and before too long, with Frank leading, somehow we had all joined in and were singing the chorus of 'Banks of the Ohio', drinking enough not to be embarrassed about it until the music took us. And later she played 'All My Trials' and took me with melancholy pleasure back to the time where I could never be again, except in dreaming moments like that one. When it was over I heard Frank tell Sheila softly that her eyes were made to cry; he said it must be the Gael in her.

After that a family of her neighbours, everyday docker folk, came in for a drink and for the kids to feed the parrots; and later we watched the movie, *Stagecoach*, on the telly, though Tusi was by then snoring prettily on the sofa. When the film was over there was a general exodus; the last thing I heard of them was Stephen's wife wanting to know where Sheila had come by her exotic Victorian loo. I had shaken hands with Frank, promising to get in touch about the bike when he was back, and got an interesting kiss from Tusi. I was getting my stuff together to leave when Sheila asked me to hang on a minute, so I was left alone in the big room while she said goodbye to them all downstairs. Then I heard her heels coming upstairs again. I stood by the fire, feeling its warmth, not really knowing what to expect. Sheila came in, smiled and walking over to me, handed me a tiny white box that had been done up in thin red ribbon. I opened it and lifted out by its chain a small silver winged M, the Matchless emblem, which she had made for me. Nothing could have pleased me more. I put it around my neck next to the skin there and then, and we sat and shared a final glass of champagne.

'I can't remember the last time I had such a good day,' I said. 'They were nice people. And I really like your place.'

'Well, buying cheap down here I had the extra money to do it up,' she said. There was a pause; then she picked up the guitar and went to hang it back on the wall, next to the long shape of a sitar, its neck fantastically ornamented with birds on the wing.

'Is that the one D. brought you back?' I asked, and when she nodded went on, 'Did you ever hear the story about that? No?

Well I don't know if I should, but it was quite a classic.'

'Go on, tell me,' she said, curling up in an armchair opposite.

'You know we moved stuff from India to the States, just once or twice? Well, one time that was how, or partly how anyway.'

'Good God,' she said, glancing at it, and I laughed and said, 'No, no, it's all gone now. But there was this old guy over there, a real craftsman who not only built the thing for us with lots of hash in place, but also put a warding spell on the case! No shit. And just as well. Denny turns up at the airport, white suit, short hair, the whole respectable bit, but he lucks out; the customs guy is a nasty, who immediately wants to open the case and maul the sitar. Denny's locked it and he's playing for time, patting himself all over for the keys, but the guy's really impatient, pulls out a clasp knife and starts to force the lock. Only somehow – the knife slips and the cat cuts himself, quite badly. There's total confusion, and the other customs guys wave Denny through.

'Now this type of drama he definitely doesn't need, because he's cut up a whole lot more stuff into bite sized cubes, wrapped each of them in clingfilm, swallowed the lot as well as a bottle and a half of kaolin and morphine to gum up his works for the flight. So sudden shocks he could do without.

'Everything goes fine till he gets to London, where he's making his flight connection to New York; it's not direct so he has to go through customs again. No trouble with the sitar that time; it was a woman at customs and she just took a very vague look at the case and passed it over, the magic was clearly in good shape. But what with the delay, and the hassles, the mixture stuff inside him wasn't working so well and just as he's standing right there in front of her he can feel a disaster beginning to occur. Which in his white suit is going to be prominent. So as nicely as he can he tells the woman the temperature is a bit chillier here than it had been back east, and could he get a sweater out of his case? She says fine, he gets it out, puts in on and pulls it down low in the nick of time, and the affected areas are covered long enough for him to make it to the gents, swallow the rest of the kaolin and morphine, and repair the damage. I met him at the far end – we were in upstate New York that time – and drove him home, then he disappeared into the bathroom with a plastic bucket for two hours. Once he'd come out and dismantled the sitar, the sun was coming up. He played a morning raga, played for hours.'

We were quiet now; I didn't know if I'd upset Sheila by alluding to what I guessed was still the man's profession. Her head was down, gazing at the fire, her long hair partially hiding her face. I cleared my throat and said, 'He did have all the moves, then. And still does, I guess. But any more nostalgia and I'll just confirm this afternoon's performance; not so much the elder statesman of flower power as just another prematurely ageing boring old fart. I'd better go and see if the bike feels willing.'

Sheila smiled, fetched my helmet and saw me out. On our way down we passed the bedroom, and I looked in once at that big platform bed. As Sheila stood in the lighted doorway watching me go through the pre-start ritual of the Matchless, I was recalling David Copperfield and asking myself, was I the hero of my own life? Because if the hero was the guy who gets the girl, Denny was definitely it.

Maybe I had something to learn from the punks after all, I thought, wincing as the bike kicked back at my first attempt to start. The lad downstairs often played one tune loud enough for me to make out the words. I kicked again. The motor stuttered into life and caught. The tune went, 'No more heroes any more'. I gave Sheila a last left-handed wave, and pulled away towards the iron bridge.

So the winter turned into more winter, the long grindingly wet and windy months after Christmas. I drove the van through a tunnel of sodium lights and neon, traffic and pedestrians' faces; only fragments stuck, and the tunnel itself which came back to me in sleep sometimes. A little girl

52

drawing back her hand calmly, and the curve of her arm before she hurled a bottle to shatter against a blank brick wall as I drove by. The guy in a suit, a little younger than me, looking at me sideways as I waited for a package and saying audibly to a colleague that he could understand why there was so much pilfering with all the types you got in and out. The fight I saw in a garage for a cause I never discovered: the smartly dressed, heavy, bear-like middle-aged man suddenly throwing sand from a fire bucket into the eyes of the guy he was quarrelling with, and jumping him from behind, looping his scarf round the other man's neck as he toppled him to the concrete floor, throttling him for a long minute while no one, myself included, intervened; as it broke up and the loud recriminations started, I was driving away. My hand knocking the glass with the first badly needed golden Special Brew all over the bar in the pub in Farringdon Street, and the thin middle-aged landlady straight away without a word replacing it for nothing.

Dream London unreeled before me; only the figures who stood over against it – the mad newslady in Kingsway, ranting and singing against the traffic noise, shouting at her customers, the perpetually smiling Chinese who served me my meals, the whimsical elderly flute-tootler in Sloane Square with his bag for contributions suspended on a string at the end of his instrument – only these stood out from the roaring flood.

In default of anything else, I learned as much as I could of the streets of London itself – every narrow lane and alley around Smithfield Market, and all the ways in and out of there; how to get from London Wall to Curzon Street in fifteen minutes in the rush hour, where to find phones that worked, the best place to park behind the Savoy, the parcels office at every main-line station, traffic lights which changed fast and those which didn't, three ways into Austin Friars in the City, when the traffic wardens were blitzing and when the dispatch riders that swarmed around St Martin's Lane and Clerkenwell were likely to be dangerously tired; I even learned to survive

53

Farringdon Road. I was nowhere near as good as a taxi driver, but better than a visitor from out of town.

One morning when I announced myself on the phone to Deborah ('This here's Rankin' Peanut'), she burst into tears. It was early; I told her to wait one, and came by the office where she was alone with flowers and a bottle, put Scotch in her coffee and we talked. The month before she had thought she was pregnant. She told her bloke; he wanted her to get rid of it. She wouldn't; he left. It had been a false alarm. I cuddled her and said if the geezer had been like that, she was well off out of it. Now it was possible I wasn't sure, but we fixed to go out together the following Friday night when we both got paid. I was seeing Sheila for a drink the day before, the Thursday. And it was that Thursday, before I met Sheila, that I took my unfinished picture to the Welsh Guards' memorial gardens, opposite the Old Bailey.

PART TWO

'Our lives dismay us. We have no comfort.
We all have dreams of leaving, everyone I know.'

David Hare, *Dreams of Leaving*

Chapter 5

Immediately after I drove away from the explosion I got stuck behind an ambulance trying to get into Farringdon Road. I didn't ask myself why it should be driving away from Bart's, just followed its jangling bell and flashing blue lights out over the stream of southbound traffic. It carried on north at Mount Pleasant. I tucked in behind and followed it all the way to King's Cross Station as it barged through the building rush-hour traffic, but there it swung left while I carried straight on, up York Way beside the back of the station until the right turn into the grubby road that housed our offices. Deborah had gone home. I handed over the packets to Blithers and got verbal for not calling in on the phone a last time; but there was no more to do, so I could get away quickly. I found that I did not mention the bombing to him. I still felt numb and confused about what I had witnessed; and now of all times was glad that I was going to see Sheila.

It was full dark by the time I reached the spot where we had arranged to meet, a quiet pub north of the Angel, near the square where I lived. She was wearing a battered brown suede coat that I had always liked, with her shining hair tucked inside its collar. I looked at her for a moment before going over. I got drinks, wine for her and a Special Brew which I took a gulp from on the way to the table.

'What's up, Jack? You look as if you need that? The traffic was terrible tonight, wasn't it; I had a job just getting here from Bethnal Green —'

'Yes. And I'll tell you the reason,' I blurted out, and launched into the whole thing. I had unconsciously lowered my voice so that our heads were close together over the small table and, when I got to the bit about it being Denny, her hand reached across the table and gripped mine as she murmured, 'No. Jack,

57

you made a mistake. You're wrong. Denny's still in Spain ... still away. It's a mistake.'

'No way,' I said. 'Now it may be coincidence, he may have had nothing to do with it, though the way it looked that's a long shot.' Her nails were biting into my hand but I finished. 'It was Denny all right.'

Sheila shook her head once; her eyes were wide as she looked around the bar and then said, 'Your place is near here, isn't it?' and when I nodded, 'Take me there.'

She followed the van in her Mini; I drove fast and we were quickly home. I parked between two bangers turning to sculpture with the rust. She came over, looking around once rather vaguely at the square and the trees in the lamplight. I let us in and led the way up the noisy stairs, feeling numb inside and obscurely excited.

Without a word we stood in my room. I had switched on the fire and a lamp and was about to say something about tea; but then I looked at her and stepping forward, leaned down and we kissed, tongues colliding in eagerness. She clung to me tightly, moaning softly; we kissed again, wild and wet, on and on. Before I knew what I was doing I had fumbled the buttons of her shirt open, unfastened her bra and slipped her breasts free, feeling her nipples erect, feeling myself stiffening too. She kissed me harder. My other hand slipped up her coat and skirt, the swelling, aching lust making me awkward at first as I pulled down her tights with a jerk and cupped her cheeks inside the soft pants, and then slipped a finger inside them to the silky hair and moist lips there.

My eyes were closed; I opened them once and said her name; she reached up to slip her tongue in my ear, while her hand squeezed and rubbed me through my jeans. All the lonely nights in that room, all the days of grind on the road and, yes, even the bodies on the street, were dissolving, yet they were the overwhelming power behind the impulse to come together with her beauty again. I was making a noise as I pushed her back on to the bed and ripped down my pants and jeans, smiling shakily at her and at my haste. She matched me, slipping off her coat, shirt and bra. I gazed again at the glory of her breasts, rounder and more perfect even than I remembered.

She slipped off the bed and, squatting in just her skirt and boots, took me in her mouth; I felt her tongue waving back and forth like seaweed over the desperately sensitive end, saw her grey-blue eyes close as I groaned. Finally I pushed her off and gently back on to the bed, and kneeling, eased off her skirt and tights and boots. I felt good now, I'd never been in such form it seemed, root rigid, hands and mouth full in all the right places at the right time, until she was moaning aloud, her neck tearing and twisting about, nipples bursting upright, cleft wet through the black silk. I reached for her pants, my thumbs hooked down each side, and slid the soft stuff over her buttocks, clasping one hand there as the other slid on with the silky black pants down her the smooth limbs, on out to her delicious bony little feet and over the pointed toes, and I flipped them away and turned back to her reverently as she lay naked on the coverlet, on her back, squirming a little, the air in the room warm, her legs bent and open like open lips, eyes closed, fair hair framing her face on the pillow, breasts tumbling.

I swung on top of her and we were kissing again and then without benefit of guiding hands I thrust up. Not viciously, but not gently either, the blood was pounding in my neck, the desperation on me. It was unerring, as it had always used to be between us; I was suddenly all the way up into the lovely warmth and softness of her. She let out a small squeal of pleasure; we thrust together once, twice, and abruptly she shouted and came, her long neck arching right back into the pillows.

I was so gorged and rigid that I felt I was never going to join her; but as we went on, with no sound but our breathing and our bellies and breasts smacking together, things seemed to keep opening out, like music in the distance that gets nearer

59

and nearer, and it ceased to be 'I moved' and 'she did that', any more than you can listen to Beethoven as a hundred separate instruments. In the oldest and truest of metaphors, we made music, and as my tip began to nudge some ultimate softness inside her, and I felt her respond, the music became gradually deeper, louder and faster, stirred, paused, swelled, more and more, swelled unbearably and then we came all at once together, came, came, came.

There had been nothing unduly athletic or complicated, considerate or controlled; but thank God there's still once or twice, for all of us, saints, sinners and the simply fucked-up, a time to let go.

Eventually the ripples subsided. Outside the window in the silence you could hear the pigeons settling for the night in the trees and in the roof above. It was my turn to lie back, feeling Sheila's head on my shoulder with her soft golden hair spilling over my chest, like so many times before.

But, of course, what had made it so good, now made it complicated. Leaving aside the business of Denny and the bombing – and mentally this was not easy to do – there was what had just happened between us. It was our previous intimacy that had allowed this deep and sudden thing; but now we both had to remember how it had ended so many times before. Still, the memory of that symphonic love was more recent, warm on our skin. So there was some uncertainty in the afterglow.

When I first tried to move she stopped me, gently, without a word. So we lay there for a while longer, and I stroked her hair and her smooth back. Finally she said simply, 'You're so kind.'

'It's my nature,' I joked; but a confusion of warm feelings were churning inside me.

'No, it isn't,' Sheila laughed. 'That's what makes it so strange. Listen, do you think I could have something to drink?'

'Sure,' I said, climbing out of bed, 'glass of wine?' and when she nodded, 'Want anything to eat? Bacon sandwich? A properly constituted bacon sandwich . . .'

'. . . Has all that is necessary to sustain human life,' she chanted, completing my old dictum parrot-fashion. 'Bacon sandwiches! You eat too much fried food, Jack. Have a look in my bag, there are some apples there.'

So I slid sideways through the minuscule kitchen door and produced a chilled bottle of Sainsbury's dry white from the fridge. I wasn't sorry she had declined the sandwich, as I was still naked, and the prospect of spattering hot fat at waist level lacked appeal. I came back to her and we sat in bed in the lamplight, drinking and nibbling sweet green apples. And, with so much between us, nothing was said; the only sound in the warm room now was the roller-blind tapping in a draught from the old low windows. I couldn't think of Denny, and both past and future seemed equally fraught. So all we could do was eat and drink a little, our bodies touching gently.

After a while Sheila shook her hair back from her face and glanced at her watch.

'Have you got a phone?' she said quietly and, when I shook my head, slipped from the bed and walked to the bathroom. When she came out she began to dress. I watched for a moment, then said, 'Stay.'

'I can't. Call me at the weekend; I'm at Stephen's on Saturday afternoon but we could meet in the evening. And, Jack —'

'Yes?'

'Don't say anything to anyone. About Denny. Will you?'

I looked her in the eyes. Then she was leaving, and I listened to her heels descending the wooden stairs, and then the front door slammed and she was gone.

Chapter 6

I stayed in bed. I was drowsy; confused but comfortable, lazily going over what had just happened, still keeping my mind firmly away from hopes for the future.

After less than an hour I heard quiet steps on the creaking stairs outside. I looked around to see if Sheila had left something and was coming back for it – nothing, so I was just reckoning it was the punk downstairs coming up to borrow a cup of glue.

Then the door splintered inwards with a crash and large men with pistols came through it, pouring fast into the room. One leapt to the bedside and held the muzzle of his gun against my temple. For a long moment the thought exploded in my head: the past, the Nutting brothers had caught up with me at last.

He was yelling – they were all making a noise – and it was a moment before I realized what the moustached face close to mine spraying saliva as it shouted was saying.

'Police! You're fucking nicked.'

Some of them stood around watching as, after they had turned out my pockets, they let me pull on my clothes as quickly as I could. Others were already going through everything in the room, tearing the spines off my books, grabbing stuff like my address book and the photos tacked beside the bed, riffling through my drawings and scattering them about the floor. I was pulling my boots on and the guys waiting were swearing at me, 'Get the cunting things on!' when a tall skinny young uniformed guy was brought in who stared at me for a moment and then nodded once and said, 'That's him.'

They took him away and, as he left, a big Alsatian, its nails clicking and slithering on the lino outside, pulled its way into the room. A sniffer-dog. This was no drug bust, I guessed, but it was a good thing I kept the doctored Coldrex at the office.

Behind the dog came a bloke with a crowbar. The last thing I saw as I was hustled out was him noisily starting to rip up the splintering floorboards. The room where I'd spent those long months was coming apart. Two more of them were crouched over the bedsheets, taking scrapings.

I was shoved down the stairs and into an unmarked car where they handcuffed me; there was an unpleasant finality to that. I didn't like the way the guys were in the car, either. There was none of that buoyancy you'd expect after they'd got a result; they were all grim, unsmiling. When the car, going fast and hard through the evening traffic, slid back on the route I'd taken from the City that afternoon, my guesses hardened to certainties. This was nothing to do with my past personal misdeeds. It was the bomb. In which some of these guys' colleagues had probably died, had definitely been maimed or disfigured. My stomach numb, I looked out of the car at the lighted shop windows and people; they could have been on another planet.

I was putting it together in my head as fast as I could, but very soon we were turning into the back entrance of the Snow Hill station, one of those gateways you scarcely notice until you've got a reason to. Under floodlights they hustled me between parked cars across the yard and in the back entrance; past the holding cells, clattering through the bad-smelling brick and iron guts of the building, everything overlaid with thick accretions of institutional paint. I was led by the same two from the car up some stairs and quickly past a large room busy with coppers, and after several more twists and turns we stopped in front of an interview room. When one of them opened the door the other shoved me sprawling inside it. The first one came in and leaned with his back against the wired-glass section of the door while the second one, bearded and burly, leisurely took off his anorak and rolled up his shirt-sleeves. I still had the handcuffs on, and I stood in the neon light against the far wall. I felt very afraid. I managed to say, 'What's this all about?'

'What's this ever-so all about, he wants to know,' sneered the guy by the door, latching on to my semi-educated accent. 'I bet you play squash, Cecil, don't you? Know how the ball bounces off the walls? Well, that's what we're going to do to you, cunt.'

Whatever happened to the hard-man and the soft-man routine, I thought, and then the bearded one stepped in, feinted so I lifted my hands, and hit me as hard as he could in the stomach. I dropped to my knees and started to retch, tears swimming in my eyes. A massive kick exploded into my backside. I was trying to scramble away, utterly humiliated, and curl up as best I could until they'd let up. But more kicks kept coming in – legs, back, the back of my head.

At ground-level I saw the bottom of the door open. A voice, far from outraged but quite incisive, said, 'That'll do.'

The kicking stopped. I scrambled to the nearest corner and got myself on my haunches facing front. A shortish middle-aged man in a three-quarter-length tweed overcoat stood just inside the door; he was carrying a manila file in one hand. The other two had backed off to the far side of the table.

'Take off the bracelets,' said the short one; his flat tones suggested a natural rather than a cultivated impassivity, with a slight London accent. So they got me up, sat me down none too gently on a chair and removed the handcuffs.

Shorty sat down opposite me and sent the maximum heavy with the rolled-up shirtsleeves away, and there were just the three of us when Shorty intoned, 'You are James Arthur Hallam?' I nodded. I had been using my own name since I had returned, and realized suddenly that no one had asked me that, or anything else, that I had not been charged, cautioned, questioned, fingerprinted or photographed. So, then, in an shaky voice, I said, since it seemed we were being civilized again, 'Yes, and I want to telephone my lawyer.'

The short one wagged his head and his forefinger in different directions. Both meant no.

'We know you're a certified naughty monkey, Jack; but you

don't know the rules on this one. Under the Prevention of Terrorism Act you can be held for up to seven days without being charged; the Act also dispenses with Judges' Rules, in case you were wondering.' Jesus, I thought, I'm back in Argentina. He went on monotonously.

'I'm Commander Kayler of the Bomb Squad; my squad's writ runs throughout the United Kingdom, and Europe as well. I'm responsible only to the Metropolitan Commissioner himself, and *he's* only answerable to the Home Secretary. This is the big time, Jack.

'Which is bad news for you. If I don't get a hundred per cent co-operation, the very least I can do to you is leave you alone with these two officers again.' The one with the moustache was giving me the hard eye, looking as if he'd enjoy that. 'What I mean by that being the very least is that I *could* let you go. Now you've no criminal record and nothing outstanding, but some of our informants tell me some friends of the Nutting brothers would make a point of looking you up if they knew you were in circulation. And we'd make sure they did know; and know exactly where to find you, too. Or we could see you went down for what happened this afternoon at the Bailey. That means fifteen to twenty years, my son; and there's a few of the Nuttings' well-wishers waiting for you inside, as well as some old-fashioned patriots.'

I didn't have to ask how they could tie me in with the bombing; I knew only too well how fingerprints had a way of magicking themselves on to compromising substances. My head and ribs ached from the brief beating, but overriding that was fear and bitterness at the position I had ended up in. After all the strokes they could have legitimately pulled me for, to get done by coincidence, while I was trying to reform, for something I knew nothing about, was choice. I remembered an old Hell's Angel adage: 'When we do right no one remembers: when we do wrong no one forgets.'

All I said was, 'What do you want to know?'

'At 5.13 this afternoon you were seen hurrying from the

scene of the explosion outside the Old Bailey, and driving away recklessly in a Ford van, registration number UMY 457S, which we have confirmed is supplied to you by your employer. One of the officers from the station noticed you and made a note of the van's registration, which is how we got your name and address.'

I had guessed that much, but it didn't explain the heavy stuff. I listened with a sick feeling as Kayler went on.

'We'd have checked you out anyway, but when we ran this through the computer it turns out you've cropped up before. You see, we know who was responsible for the bombing this afternoon. How we know is none of your concern, but we do. And it turns out you've been best friends with him since schoolyard days, and just recently you've been seeing a lot of his girlfriend . . .'

I gave it a try.

'Who's that?' I asked.

The heavy-knuckled slap shook the teeth in my mouth. Kayler must have signalled the moustache to let go at me, but I'd missed it. When my eyes focused again he had an air of mild reproach, as like a conjuror his fingers extracted a photograph from the file in his hand. It was the picture I had had tacked to the shelf by my bed, me and Denny smiling in the long-past Cornish sunlight.

'Dennis Lee, that's who. Now tell us, chummy, how you helped him at the Old Bailey today while he was performing.'

'It's true I was there, but it was just a coincidence . . .' As the words were out I could hear how thin they sounded. 'And I haven't seen Denny for about ten years.'

'That's a lie, Jack. For a start you saw him this afternoon at the Bailey.'

'If you say so. But I didn't recognize him.'

'You didn't see him ride past, on a bike like the one in this picture?' Kayler said quizzically, tapping the photo.

'I saw a bike, a red and white Trident, turning right across the traffic just before the bomb went off,' I said. 'But I didn't recognize the rider.'

I tensed, expecting another blow. Kayler just looked at me. In his frown of concentration I recognized the policeman's hallmark: the certainty of right and wrong. He was not a nice man, not someone you could tell your troubles to or whom you would expect to place anything but the harshest interpretation on your actions. As well as which, he definitely wasn't stupid. So for whatever reason I was not admitting to recognizing Denny, I had to do it convincingly.

'If it was Dennis Lee,' I repeated, 'I didn't recognize him. Whoever was riding had on leathers and a full-faced helmet. It was dusk; they were moving very fast, really shifting. It was a Triumph all right but someone doing what he was would scarcely use their own machine, would they? And how did you even know the rider was the one that threw the bomb? And you're wrong about how friendly we were in the old days. He's not a guy I particularly remember. I kept the picture because of the bikes in it.'

Kayler kept his eyes on me while he said, 'We've found the bike already; it was stolen, but it's his kind of thing, and two of our men saw the rider slap a charge on the door of the Judge's Rolls.' He pulled out another sheaf of papers from his folder, and only dropped his gaze when he started reading from them in a flat monotonous drone.

' "... when you're that close to someone it can be hard to see them clear. It was like he was a part of me; maybe that's why I'd so like to get in touch with him again, it would be sort of like getting in touch with a part of myself ... I don't know. In real terms he was always brighter than me ..." Et cetera, et cetera, et cetera,' he concluded, dropping the papers back into the file. 'Are you going to deny you said all that?'

It was like the moment when they started hitting me, only in a way worse. I realized it was a transcript of a recording, that Sheila's place was bugged, that she was already involved and their grasp of things was that extensive, that it was all that serious. As I sat stunned Kayler bored in, exploiting the moment of weakness.

'You knew him all right, you little shit. Now tell us your part in today, and tell us where he is now. If not, you go down for him.'

'No,' I said, 'No. Listen. Remember on what you just read. I was saying I'd like to get in touch with him again. I didn't know anyone was listening but friends and that's what I said. And it's true.'

'Oh no. That's what you would say to other people if you were seeing him and up to your neck in this.' Now Kayler's knuckles were whitening on the file, but the monotone scarcely varied as he gestured with his other hand.

'Over there in Bart's they've got extra doctors, volunteers from other places, still sewing people up. There are a lot of burns, too; the explosive in the bomb was the kind that produced a high temperature, and so there were flash burns. A lot of them are going to need plastic surgery in the long term. And that's the minor stuff. In surgery they've used pints of blood in double figures on just one person alone, the woman who was a passenger in the car next to the Judge's Rolls; and she lost a leg because they had to leave her and operate on a man with internal injuries so bad they were *manipulating* his insides, his liver.

'The copper who was standing close by, his lungs are damaged so they're filling like a sponge, with blood instead of air. They've helicoptered him to the Accident Hospital at Birmingham where they've got a new lung by-pass machine, but they don't know yet if he'll live. Another copper had a foot blown off and the one in the car behind, both his eyes were cut by flying glass, and he's lost the use of them for good. The Judge died – the man I was supposed to be protecting – and so did his driver and the driver of the car next to him. There's a code to let us know about bombs; but if they were determined I suppose they could have proxy-bombed the Judge's motor with him in it while it was still inside, out of harm's way. But to make a point they had to do this cowboy job outside the Bailey, in a busy street with no warning.

'Now, you tell me about Dennis Lee.'

Chapter 7

It was ten o'clock, and the start of a long night for us all. I stuck
to my story, that is, the truth, minus the fact that I had recognized Denny; they seemed to be convinced it was him anyhow, presumably on a tip-off and, having initially recoiled
from the idea of pointing the finger at Denny, I now had to
stick to it for my own sake.

So we went up, down and sideways: about my movements
during the day, my contacts with Sheila, with radical movements in the past, even with trade unions, and the whole
history of my friendship with Denny. This was awkward: they
had the story about running the dope on tape and I couldn't
remember how much I'd said about being involved; but they
already knew me on form for a dealer, and if I hesitated now it
looked like covering up and brought down what I came to
dread more than physical punishment, the hectoring, bullying,
absolute certainty on their part that I was a despicable and
untrustworthy liar. And, as the night wore on, I began to be
infected with their bad opinion of me, to share of it, and
several times caught myself on the brink not just of admitting
what I knew, but of fabricating more evidence, implicating
myself more thoroughly. That was how strongly I thought
they were right.

They kept on and on. Kayler was called away several times
but others spelled him. They had coffee, or came back with
washed hands and faces, smelling of soap, but there was none
of that for me, and no toilet trips either. The original two
heavies were still around, though there was only one more bit
of physical nastiness, and that was also the moment I got my
feet badly tangled. From taking my flat to pieces they knew I
had been with a woman shortly before they had got hold of
me. When this was first brought up I tried to say it was a
pick-up from the pub, someone I'd never seen before. I even

invented a name for her, Veronica. They looked at me and were quite rightly sceptical. While we went over the rest of the day yet again they must have sent men round to the pub with my picture, got the landlord up and checked out the story; only they had also thought to take along a picture they had from the surveillance team of Sheila, and the landlord identified her as the girl I had left with.

When this piece of information was brought to the harshly lit, bad-smelling, smoky room in the middle of the night, the one with a moustache rose and with one motion kicked the chair out from under me. I was unprepared and went down hard, and as I sprawled on the floor he stood over me with his foot drawn back, shouting, 'Celebrating, were you? Giving her one to celebrate?' until a word from Kayler called him off. So then I had to admit that I had been with Sheila, and having been caught in a lie once, my whole story was called into question, and we were off again. I knew their game: confuse you, spin you around, scare you silly until you say what they want to hear. I knew what they were doing, but I also had to admit it was working.

Once again we went over the gathering at Christmas and the things that were said about Denny. I thought they would be hot on to Frank McMillen, being Irish, but surprisingly they didn't pursue that end of things. They knew from the tapes that he had met Denny but, once I had said several times that I hadn't seen him before or since that Christmas Day, they let it go. The piece of paper with his phone number on it was stuck in my address book with no name attached; they didn't ask so I didn't tell them. It might be something I could use with them later.

But curiosity about it all finally prompted me to ask Kayler a question. It was the middle of the night; the room was sound-proofed, killing any noise from the corridor outside, and there was a lull in the interrogation as Kayler sipped at a plastic cup of coffee, its aroma reaching me. In the silence I looked across at him blearily and said what came into my head.

71

'But it was the Irish, surely? The Judge had just sent down a bunch of IRA men. What's Denny got to do with the Irish?'

Kayler gave me a measured look and finally said, 'All right, let's pretend you don't know. When your girlfriend told you Lee was away, where did you think he was? What did you think he was doing?'

'Like I told you, she never said,' I answered, 'so I always thought he was, you know, still into moving dope maybe. But she never said, one way or the other, and I never asked.'

'Well, you'd have been wrong,' said Kayler. 'He was in France and Spain, in the Pyrenees, working with the ETA, the Basque terrorists.'

I couldn't answer. It was one more thing to digest and I felt I had reached the overload point. They could easily be wrong or lying but if so my head was too scrambled to work out why, or what it meant if they were. I kept my eyes down. Unexpectedly Kayler turned round to someone in the shadows behind him and said, 'All right, you can take him down now.'

Just like that. It was over, or seemed to be, for the moment. Without another word I was led stumbling out of that room and back down the way I had come to the holding cells. We stopped outside one, they took my bootlaces and belt, then the keys rattled as they unlocked it and they gestured for me to go in. After I had stepped inside, the door slammed like a bomb exploding behind me. The keys rattled again as they banged me up, and I was alone.

The light came from one bare bulb behind a wire mesh. There was a plain narrow wooden bunk, worn smooth, bolted like a bench to the wall. The only other furniture was a lavatory in one corner with no seat, just a wooden strip screwed to the rim and no chain. The walls were tiled like an old-fashioned public lavatory. There was no window and no heating, and the whole place smelled like school used to, only worse – disinfectant and staleness, conveying boredom and fear.

I sat on the bench with my back pressed to the tiled wall.

Outside in the corridor there was intermittent, ceaseless thumping, jingling, clattering. I was very tired but at first completely tense with apprehension; every time the sounds came outside I was convinced that they had simply brought me down here to give me a serious going-over away from prying eyes. There seemed to be no one in the cells on either side.

But, eventually, between monotony and weariness I calmed down. I still could not sleep and I used the time to think. I didn't even bother to consider putting the fix in with them – I had little money and few friends, and on this one it wouldn't do anyhow. So what did they want?

Denny – they seemed convinced it was him, and it did look that way. But, failing Denny, they wanted a body to go down for the bombing; so that was me. I knew it hadn't been just idle chatter about fitting me up for it. As a response to what I had seen in the street that afternoon, I could even understand it.

No, I had been wrong; this wasn't Argentina. There would be no disappearance, no bullet in the back of the neck. Instead I would be left screaming soundlessly behind that glass wall that all prisoners and deviants know; unable to convince anybody that authority is not only incompetent and evasive, but dishonest – they can do what they like and nearly always get away with it, and they *will* do it, to get their way. I could visualize vividly the sorry train of events from there on in: imprisonment, legal process, sentencing, then the personal and impersonal violence and the deprivation inside. I doubted absolutely whether I had the strength to bear it. From then on I would never know what was going to happen to me from minute to minute, because it would all be up to someone else, and it wasn't in their interests to tell me. Just like then and there in that cell.

All this for Denny? For someone who had done what I had seen out in the street? Well, not quite. For a start I didn't know for sure it was him, though between me and them it looked pretty conclusive. But, if so, he had changed; in the past Denny had been radical enough in his thinking, but rarely violent.

Then, involuntarily, I smiled. Denny would probably say the same about me – Jack? he's wide, but not vicious – and, despite the self-defence element, the killings which I had been responsible for in the last ten years would have come as a surprise to him.

I shrugged; leaving that out, leaving out his motives – and maybe there was an angle, maybe the Irish had something on him to make him do it – if he *had* done it, I was not going to shop him, and equally I was not going to have anything to do with him ever again. But I wasn't going to let him, or the law, drag Sheila into this any further than she was already, if there was anything I could do to prevent it. Of her innocence I was sure. I clung to it; and, even in that grim place, once or twice the thought of her, though infinitely distant and painful, gave me strength and even a brief happiness. It seemed we had no future now – we probably never did have – but I told myself there was nothing I wouldn't do for her.

I had no way of knowing how long had passed, or what time it was, when without warning the door slammed open. I stayed sitting on the bunk. Kayler stood outlined for a moment in the doorway then walked in, with his moustached guard-dog at his side. The cell door closed behind them.

'All right, Jack,' said Kayler monotonously. 'Listen, and listen carefully. We're letting you go.'

I couldn't stop myself; I started to thank him. His cold stare and weary headshake stopped me as he went on.

'No, no, you're not off the hook; this is only the beginning. I want that bastard Lee, and you're my way to him. He doesn't know we know; he may be in touch with the girl and, if he is, you'll find out. If we pull her in now, we lose that way to him. With you there, we're in with a chance.'

'Yeah,' growled Moustache. 'If she's dropping her knickers for you, she might tell you something next time you're getting tore up her.'

I ignored him and asked Kayler, 'What about whoever says he did it? If they know so much, don't they know where he's at? '

'Never heard of a closed cell?' said Kayler. 'Your friend's a paid-up urban guerrilla now. He don't go around handing out his address to no one.

'If you get us Lee, you might, just might, come through this. We found your picture in the gardens where you said it was. I ain't saying I believe you, but there's an off-chance you were more stupid than bent this time. But we'll never be far away, and there's nowhere you can run to. And, if I even think you're pulling anything tricky, I'll either have you or turn you over to the Nuttings' pals. And that's a promise, Jack.'

Chapter 8

Ten minutes later I was out on the street, in the chill dawn by Holborn Viaduct. It was about quarter past six; I knew because my watch was back on my wrist, and the money and van keys in my pocket. I turned up my jacket collar against the chill dawn wind and walked down the empty road to where they had parked the van. I unlocked it and slid behind the wheel. The windows of the hamburger place opposite, blown out by the explosion, were boarded up crudely with cardboard; the newsvendor's placard read, 'THREE DIE IN OLD BAILEY TERROR BOMB'. Shards of broken glass were piled in the gutter, the familiar urban signal of disaster.

Sitting in the van felt like home, felt secure again, but I knew it was an illusion; they'd have guys on me, probably at least a three-car team, and almost certainly there would be a bleeper attached to the van somewhere. There was nowhere to run, Kayler had said, and outwardly I was going to act as if I agreed with him. But in my head there were some very different notions.

Technically, the past night had never happened. I wasn't on any kind of record except Kayler's private one as having been picked up, processed or spent time there. They'd said the flat had been put back to rights and, if the neighbours were curious, I could laugh it off as a bad case of mistaken identity; the idea was to keep the news of my contact with the police away from Sheila and, by extension, Denny.

But I was off and running now, and both instinct and experience told me to follow my feelings as well as my head; and after the bust I had a strong resistance against returning to the flat again. It was as if some pervert burglar had crapped on the carpet. Besides, the stuff I really needed now wasn't there.

But first things first. Bar Sheila's apple, I hadn't eaten since lunch the day before, or washed since we'd been in bed. So I started up and drove the short way through the early morning streets to Mount Pleasant, and in a large, old-fashioned café, crowded with dull-faced postal workers, hungrily gulped down a big fried breakfast and three cups of sweet tea. Next I drove to King's Cross Station and at the chemists there bought a toothbrush, shaving things and a pair of scissors; then went up York Way to our office, where I let myself in and used the grungy communal toilet and wash-basin, which the courier firm shared with the rest of the building, to clean up in as best I could. It was not yet nine thirty, and neither Blithers or Deborah had arrived yet. I made myself a coffee, took it to the top-floor office and drank, washing down a couple of my doctored Coldrex capsules with the last of it. I looked at the phone for a while, but there was no way I could risk ringing Sheila's bugged house. Next to the phone on the desk was a cash box; I got the key from where I knew Deborah kept it and helped myself to my wages which were packeted up inside. I could feel the speed starting to tingle as I zipped the wages into my jacket pocket along with the toilet stuff and the uppers, and bounced down the stairs, back to the van and out into the rush hour for a couple of regular early calls. Kayler had told me to carry on as normal until I had made contact with Sheila as we had arranged. By now, with the empty streets earlier, I was pretty sure that a green Ford van was one of my shadows; but I knew I couldn't rely on making them all.

Within minutes I was sweating heavily, stopping and starting in the thick traffic, heading down towards an ad agency in Covent Garden. I looked out at the metal stream and the fraught faces, and felt a daily diatribe building up inside me against their race, ancestry and driving habits, their looks, tastes, and the fact that they were caught like me – oh yes, by the middle of the day I was usually ranting to myself aloud. I hated them even more now for what they didn't know – they were like those films of herds of game, curiously indifferent to the predators, the violence and death that moved among them. It came to me how much I hated the city now, how ready I was to crack out of it. I had switched on the radio in the van; the bombing was still in the news, and I could imagine the urgency building up for Kayler to get a result. Later the imbecile who orchestrated the capital's awakening commented on a photo in the papers that morning taken at the scene of the explosion minutes after it had happened, a close-up of a policeman's grief-stricken face as he helped his injured friends.

'Great picture,' said the DJ, 'pity it's such a drag subject.'

By ten I was calling the office for orders. Deborah and Blithers were both there, a fact for which I was quietly grateful, as in front of him, by unspoken agreement, Deborah and I had never mentioned the fact that we were planning to see each other, and so didn't do so now; it may have been paranoia, but I didn't know who could be listening. I told them about dropping by for the wages, pleading extreme poverty. And so the day went on. It was strange weather for February, close, almost opressively warm, but with intermittent drizzle covering the street with a fine coating of wet mud; and, being a Friday, the traffic was up. I bounced around, from Soho to Aldgate, London Wall to Parliament Square. My back ached from its bruises; my head was wound up tight with the speed, the strain of pushing through the traffic and the thought of what was to come. Stopped in a line of cars or at the lights, my hands would pound the wheel compulsively, trying to dredge up a beat, a rhythm to carry me through this.

I made stops, in between calls, at random. A bank in Clerkenwell Road where I drew out extra money. A clothes shop at one end of Fleet Street where I bought a pale blue shirt and a light-grey tracksuit top. A pub in Fitzrovia for lunch, with an evening paper for company; the amphetamine meant I hadn't much appetite, and I stayed off the Special Brew, but drank down two pints of lager against the dry mouth and parched lips the sulphate caused. Then took another couple of pills.

Since it had never really got light, you hardly noticed it when above the lamps the lowering, muddy sky began to darken still further. Despite it, I was sweating even more freely than before, stumbling and stuttering over my words with receptionists and dispatchers. One of the girls I dealt with in Knightsbridge said to her colleagues, 'Hurry up. I think the courier's getting emotional.' I rewarded her with a sickly smile.

By then it was half past five. I checked on the phone, which Blithers answered, Deborah already having left as I had hoped. So I set off back towards Hyde Park Corner, intending to turn left off it into Park Lane and Edgware Road, and from there to Marylebone Road, where I was going to run my number. But the Friday night exodus was thick and clogging and, as I approached Hyde Park Corner, I liked what I saw ahead. Dithering in the left lane until the last moment, I finally heeled off to the right and down the underpass beneath the madness of the Corner itself. Since the traffic was slow moving, starting and stopping, it was no great feat; but I was hoping whoever was ahead of me would have been seduced into the traffic circling Hyde Park Corner. I had already clocked the green van four cars behind; I even knew his registration number by now, and the face of the driver, who was on his own.

The cars ground along in the tall, fume-filled, beige-coloured curved tunnel, brake-lights flashing on and off as they shuttled forwards, halted or freed by the lights and thick traffic in Piccadilly, which I knew would be packed as usual. I had put my leather jacket on and zipped it up before starting for Knightsbridge and I stuffed the plastic bag with the clothes I had bought that morning down the front. The curved tunnel began to rise. For a sickening moment I thought the traffic was going to keep moving and let us up and out. But then it slowed and brake-lights flared ahead. I found I was trembling violently now.

Finally the car in front came to a halt. I jerked on the hand-brake and switched off the engine with my left hand while swinging the door open with my right. I left the car in a crouch under the incredulous eyes of the outside lane of traffic which had started to move slowly. I slipped the door closed behind me and, bent double, began to scuttle up the side of the row of grunting, grumbling cars ahead, through the fume-laden air towards the high cave-mouth of the tunnel and the wet night air ahead. Behind the first horns began to blare. I ducked in front of the car on my left just as it began to move, and then straightened and sprinted out along beside the line of moving cars, out on to the raised pavement and into the night.

All around the Hyde Park Corner madness was in full swing, with traffic coming round from the Knightsbridge direction playing 'Who's-going-to-give-way-first?' with the three lanes streaming in from the left from Park Lane. I ran off the dividing pavement into the middle of all this without breaking step. It was all lights, the dazzle of headlights in the dark, the slash of red tail-lights; a horn blared close but mostly pedestrian lunacy was given its due, and I was halfway across, jinking and weaving but never breaking pace, when a car coming from Park Lane, seeing the traffic slowing for me, but not seeing me, grabbed the opportunity and shot forward straight at me.

His brakes squealed. I was up in the air, leaping, jumping clear, with one hand on his wing to fend him off and get clear. Pain shot through my wrist but I kept going, landing awkwardly, using a foot on the bumper of a car stalled in front to kick off from and sprint across the last few yards, over the bus lane, vaulted the railings and I was running fast up Picca-dilly, blowing hard, brushing startled pedestrians in front as I finally skidded left around the corner and up towards Shepherd's Market, and halfway up the next street ducked into the back entrance to the NCP car-park building there, took the steps three at a time and finally stopped on the passage to the second storey, standing gulping for breath, heart pounding, listening for pursuit. I hadn't looked back once.

There was nothing, just the echoing noises of the car-park. With shaking hands I pulled off my black jacket, took out the light-grey top and put it on; I bundled the jacket into the plastic bag which the new clothes had come in and loped off down the steps towards the car-park's front entrance; and from there to Curzon Street and, on the corner of it, the most comfortable cinema in London.

Deborah shrieked when she saw me, but the Stockwell fun palace of a pub where she had chosen to meet me covered up the sound. It could have been the model for 'Sultans of Swing'; a Dixieland jazz band was giving its syncopated all, blaring out above a normally animated South London Friday night.

What made her shriek was that, first, during the performance at the Curzon, I had cut and then shaved off my beard in the cinema's well-appointed gentlemen's cloakroom; and later I had worked my way on foot up to Wardour Street in Soho and, after a detour, visited a hairdresser's there which stayed open late and had them give me a fashionable short back and sides before catching a Victoria Line tube down to our rendezvous. As Deborah gaped, I shrugged and said, 'It was time for a change.' Her expression suggested that maybe it hadn't been a change for the better, but she grinned and let me buy her a drink. I had clocked the clientele carefully on my way in and everything seemed all right. I'd done some more speed as well and the music, fast and loud, seemed just right; I gulped down Special Brew feeling taut and good. Whatever shit was going down all around me, for tonight I was moving again. My thinking was that while the fuzz would have my description, Kayler wouldn't go public with it for fear of scaring off Denny and, as he would think, Sheila. So if I could stay out of the filth's hands, I was in with a chance.

I took Deborah back her Martini and slid on to a seat beside her. She was looking good in a black velour V-necked top and black pencil skirt under her mac. I kissed her casually and moved up so we were pressed together on the seat and I was close against her rather large, well-built body. There were no objections. I didn't think too closely about what I was going to do, what I might be letting her in for; I just did it.

'Blithers on form today?'

'Going on a bit. As usual.' Not half as much as he'd be going on now, I thought, after he's discovered his van full of packages was stuck firmly in the Hyde Park underpass and his ace driver had done a runner.

'If I had my druthers,' I said, 'I'd druther be Ranking Peanut than that asshole. Thank God it's Friday.'

We drank some more, moaned about work and discussed my new image, talking loud and fast against the prevailing musical bedlam. After another round it seemed quite natural for me to say, 'You doing anything this weekend?'

She looked me in the eye as she shook her head.

'Well, listen, where did you say your folks live?'

'Down in Cornwall,' she said, puzzled. 'The other side of Camborne. But I haven't been back since last summer.'

'Well, how about it?' I said. 'This city's bringing me right down. How would you like to go home for the weekend?'

'What?'

'Do it. Go home. Drive down there, right away, tonight. I haven't got the van and it's a bit wet for the bike, but we could take your pregnant rollerskate' (this was Trucker for her VW Beetle). 'I wouldn't hassle your folks, I've got mates down that way I can stay with. I'll drive too; I don't just drive for a living, I really get off on it. Let's just do it, what do you say? Together we'll knock 'em over.'

'I thought,' she said slowly, 'we might be spending some time together up here . . .'

'Some rather fascinating things,' I replied distinctly, 'once happened to me in the back of a Volkswagen.'

She held my gaze with her marvellous dark pensive eyes for a beat, and then exploded into laughter.

'OK, yes, pository,' she spluttered, and I grabbed her and kissed her, and leapt up to get more drinks in celebration.

I was not eager to leave yet so we stayed, in fact until chucking out, by which time I was on to halves of lager with whisky chasers; Deborah, it seemed, could soak up Martini like blotting paper with no visible effect. I bought a six-pack of lager from the bar as we left; then, clutching my plastic bag of belongings, shambled out into the damp night air, palming a couple more pills as I popped the first can while waiting for her to unlock the rollerskate. But, standing there, I was brought up short by the sight of the Beetle's seats; they both had black sheepskin covers and were tilted forward, the dark shapes slumped over the dash like dead men. I was feeling a slight giddiness as the capsules slid down my throat on a breaking wave of golden beer; this was complete fucking madness, but in view of the events of the last thirty-six hours, it seemed to be the only way to go.

In the car I got behind the wheel, stuck the open can in the side pocket of my door and undid a window so she could slam hers; I had ridden in a lot of Beetles, and they're all air-tight, though the late-engaging clutch still managed to surprise me. We belted up. Without a word she stuck a cassette in the stereo deck and bang on cue Bruce Springsteen's 'Born to Run' began to wail. I took a stick of gum and a mouthful of beer and, feeling like South London's answer to Neal Cassady, wheeled her on out.

Chapter 9

The only trouble was, I might be feeling good enough, but I was seeing double; though sufficiently together to make sure it was the off-side eye I shut, so that Deborah didn't see me driving through London like a demented voluntary Moshe Dayan.

As we negotiated the Friday night traffic to Clapham Common, cut through Putney, across Barnes, and clattered over the narrow iron bridge at Hammersmith, Deborah sat huddled up in her mac digging the music, quietly excited about the journey and getting back home. Up on the elevated two-lane after Chiswick I was still seeing double, the traffic swishing and creeping all around. The little car pulled well, clattering along steadily; the clock towers on the factories below told me it was close to midnight but, as we came to the end of the two-lane and saw it fanning out to the width of the M4 proper, all three lanes were full of red tail-lights moving steadily away from London, electrical mechanical rodents sliding from the foundering city.

We needed petrol, and the conviction had been growing in the last hour that, despite the pills, I also needed some food and sit-down if I was going to handle another 300 miles that night. So ignoring possible surveillance, we hit the second gin palace of the evening – Heston Services, the tawdry gateway to the holy body of the west. In the near empty cafeteria Deborah toyed with an egg and chips while I happily went the whole route on skinless sausages, pallid tomatoes, two rubbery eggs and a heap of greasy Krinkle-Kuts washed down with a grimy, watery sludge they put out as coffee. It tasted good to me. I shovelled it down, Deborah keeping her eyes tactfully averted. I was not proud of my drunkard's appetite, even then; and I was grateful for the way she didn't hassle, how quiet she was.

But, as an Argentine friend used to say, who knows what voices they are hearing?

We filled up with three-star under the arc lights, and I went to check the oil and tyres. Straightening up with the gauge from the first wheel, I saw a white, orange-striped, police Cortina parked by some railings about forty yards away. It was impossible to judge whether the two dark shapes inside were staring at us or not. Feeling acutely exposed I finished on the wheels and slid behind the steering wheel; I switched on and we drove past them steadily and down on to the motorway again. From the darkness Deborah's voice said, 'That could have been awkward, if they'd stopped us.'

'Yeah,' I said. 'I feel better now though, after the food. You know my favourite drunk-driving story? Apparently one time in the thirties some titled lady was completely bombed, really out of it, and at the wheel of something pre-war and fast, with her grown-up son for a passenger. After about ten minutes he couldn't take it any more, so he asked, ultra-polite, would she like him to drive? All she said was, "I thought you were".'

The traffic had thinned out after that nicely final sign, 'No Services For 56 Miles', and when the overhead lights stopped we were into the tunnel of the night, hitting a steady eighty in the middle lane. There was softer music, Joni Mitchell, on the tape now. Nothing passed us and I opened the side windows a crack further, zipped up my jacket and settled to it, double vision gone, Deborah a dim shape huddled in her mac in the glow of the dash-lights. Despite occasional hits on the beer can to moisten my throat, my mind was clearer too; I figured night moves while playing the aviator to keep alert, concentrating on the figures on the road-signs, the mileage on the clock, the petrol gauge and the luminous face of my watch. The motor-way went on and on; we moved through the darkness.

Until Bristol and, again, clover-leaves and loops of orange sodium lamp-lit emptiness, and I was at that peculiar tingling edge of awareness, the fine edge between energy and fatigue, where I felt it all, the emptiness but also the abstraction of the highway, the swells and curves of the road as pure design even while we were riding on a part of it; as well as the impersonal hugeness, the Bug just that, a bug indeed, an amoeba in the veins of the country's body; but if the veins were concrete, the country no body maybe, but metamorphosing, petrifying chunk by concrete chunk into some new creation, a fit habitation for machines, say, for the cars and bikes I loved and lived in; for machines and drivers like me, for magazine-reading robots? And maybe that was what Denny was trying to blow apart.

I wasn't so high that I didn't clock the second police car of the night, stationary on a raised hump by the side of the road ahead of us, and adjusted our speed accordingly. I decided it was time to get off the motorway. I said to Deborah, 'This super-slab shit is boring. I'm going to switch on to the A-roads down to Exeter; is that OK?'

'Fine,' she said, 'you're the driver. Let me know when you're getting tired and I'll take over.'

I turned off to the left at Junction 19 just below the long bridge over the Avon, drove past the services there, did the five miles or so until we hit the A38 and turned on to it, heading south.

Deborah had begun to doze. We were mounting a rise on the southern outskirts, hitting about sixty on a long fairly steep uphill left-hand curve, when I saw a car ahead in a turning off to the left, stationary, and then beginning to move into the main road.

Inexplicably, because he must have seen us, but he was moving right out in front of us. As he flickered closer I had time to wrench the wheel and get out about half of a high-pitched exclamation compounded of 'Shit!' and 'Jesus!' when at the back there was the lightest of bumps, the faintest impact imaginable and we were driving on unscathed. Paranoid alarm bells were going off in my head. Had someone got on me, was that an attempt to stop us? But the other guy was quickly lost in the rear-view mirror and there was no pursuit. But though

Deborah had woken, it had happened too quick for her and, soon, for me, to take seriously.

'We used to come down this way from Bristol on bikes in the old days,' I told her. 'Bridgwater, Taunton, Wellington.' The 'we' was me and Denny. In that way it was a journey back into the past.

'We hitched to Camborne down the A30 from London one weekend,' said Deborah, 'and we got picked up by this guy in an MG who ended up taking us all the way. It turned out he wasn't really going west, or anywhere in particular – he just spent his weekends travelling around, on the road. A bit like us, I suppose.' I guess the 'we' in her story was her and the boy-friend. For the first time I wondered if she was thinking of him much, if it bothered her.

The road was emptied now by the motorway and the night, but after the M4 the winding roads and sleeping villages needed concentration, as I was still kicking along as fast as I could go. Beyond Wellington, fatigue was beginning to bite; I had nodded a couple of times and my braking was getting erratic. Also flatulence from all that gassy lager and fried food was becoming a bit of an embarrassment. Finally, with Deborah huddled up dozing in the corner, I could contain it no longer and the sound of a ripe fart cut the stale air of the car. From the corner a voice sweetly recited:

'A fart is good at any time
It gives the body ease
It warms the bed in winter time,
And makes music for the fleas.'

'Well,' I grunted, 'what do you think they call us breakers for?'

By the time we reached Exeter it was nearly half past three in the morning and we'd done almost two hundred miles. We passed the Black Horse Café and plunged under the motorway; drove through the town and on the hill above rejoined the dual carriageway, the A38 again, heading west. There were repairs going on to the surface, and every so often the road would narrow and switch through mud-slippery channels lined with red and white plastic tags, to emerge on the opposite side of the carriageway, now three-lane two-way, until a few miles further along the same thing would happen again and we would be switched back to the proper side.

It had been raining, and I had steadied down to seventy now. We were slogging on over the big undulating hills, about twenty miles from Plymouth and the bridge over the Tamar into Cornwall, running down one of these three-lane sections, when there was a flash of lights in the mirror, coming up fast and undipped. As I ducked my head in the dazzle I caught a glimpse of red and white barrels and signs, where the road narrowed and switched back to the other side again. Before I knew what I was doing I had my foot in the tank; whoever it was, there was no way I was sitting there to be cut up and slowed down, as well as dazzled, before we reached the cross-over.

Slowly the clock climbed, here was where you really felt the Beetle's lack of urge, eighty-two, eighty-three and he was nearly alongside, in my blind spot, ahead the arrows and barrels sliding closer; someone had to brake and it couldn't be me, not with the mud and the way the tail-engined Bug could spin. I couldn't brake hard enough to let him through and I knew it even as I saw his nose edging slowly up on the outside. I sucked in breath sharp, he was too close, this was *it*.

Just as I gasped he began to fall away, and with a second to spare I started dabbing at the brakes, slamming down into third at the last minute, barrels zipping by on both sides. I still thought we'd probably plough into one where the lane kinked; as I let the clutch out in third, I felt our back end begin to wobble and we half mud-slid through the bend, an inadvertently natty fish-tail, and then we were clear and running, up through the gears again, the dazzling lights still behind.

Incredibly Deborah was sleeping through it all. Again I had

time to wonder, with a stab of realization, if this might be more than a street race. I hadn't made out any conical lights silhouetted on top of the car behind, so I simply did what I could, kept my foot right down and led the bastards until the last big hill before Plymouth. Then the lights behind crept up closer again; the VW's sorry gearing let me down on the long climb and just over the crest he had me, tearing by, doing well over the ton. I saw the back seat full of heads and imagined the lads chortling as they swooped down the hill; round red tail-lights, a CND sign upside down, an old Cortina, of course.

We'd done our little number but, though I was getting a bit worried about petrol now, I didn't exactly slow down; my neck was stiff with tension and I was eager for the bridge and the beginning of the last lap.

We came down the hill towards the big roundabout before Plymouth. Beside me Deborah shifted and yawned.

'Good sleep?' I asked. 'Sweet dreams?'

She giggled and said throatily, 'Yes. I dreamt my behind was a sugar lump, and you were sucking it.' Her hand squeezed my thigh, then slid higher. I squeaked and said, 'Baby, you're racing my motor.'

True to my words, within about a minute we were doing seventy along the middle of the tilted road around the top of Plymouth, with the crash barrier zipping by outside. And it was then I caught sight of a blue light in the mirror.

It was the evening's Third Policeman, and I found time to curse them for missing the Cortina we had raced and picking up on me. Then I was stationary and trembling by the roadside, murmuring to Deborah, 'Fuzz,' trying to sound as casual as if I was announcing the arrival of the milkman; but my mind full of the prospect of Kayler's retribution and cursing my 'Drive On Through' bullshit which had led to this, getting pulled for speeding. I watched them in the mirror getting out each side, slowly, as usual, adjusting their caps.

I jumped out as they approached. In my haste to slam the door the seat belt got caught in it and it shot open again, beer from the open can stuck in the door's side pocket sheeting upwards and landing with a flat splash on the pavement. So I was standing in a puddle of booze, leaning back on the door which still wouldn't shut, as I bade them a tremulous good evening.

'I mean, seventy-five through the town?' was all the first one said; young, fair-haired, perplexed rather than exasperated. 'I mean, it may be the middle of the night, but over seventy?'

Abject submissiveness. Behavioural science endorses this as the only way to deal with such a situation. It came naturally, too. I nodded, an eloquently all-admitting gesture, and said I was sorry. After all, they call themselves 'Your Friendly Devon and Cornwall Fuzz'; though that hadn't been my experience when we had come through on the bikes ten years ago.

'You were doing seventy-five in a thirty-mile limit, my cock,' said the second one. Here we had the heavy, a crop-headed squaddy with a Cornish chin and nothing but busting on his mind.

If they recognized me, or asked me for my documents and recognized the name from the alert which I had to think was out, I was done for. Or if they went through the car. There was a long moment's silence; I was uneasily aware of the flat smell of stale beer wafting upwards from the pavement.

Finally the fair-haired one said, 'Well, where are you going?'

And I couldn't even answer that. I wasn't about to reveal my own destination and I had forgotten where Deborah came from. All I could say was, 'I'm taking her home,' and then the door pushed open behind me and Deborah leaned over, smiling gravely as she looked up at them and said the name of the village where she lived.

A miracle. The dark-haired one, ignoring the can in the door, said, 'My Uncle Arthur and his boy live up there, my dear.'

'You mean Arthur Goodman? Then I went to school with your cousin. Did you know he got engaged last month?'

'No! Did he? Who is she?'

Five minutes later we were rolling across the high toll bridge over the Tamar in the dark above the water, the cross-wind shoving at the little car. I had whooped with relief as we pulled away from the cops, then given Deborah a quick hug of gratitude.

'I go to jelly at a time like that,' I explained; but coincidence and momentum had carried us through and I drove on, fumbling in my bag for a fresh beer, palming another tab of speed as I did so, drinking and swallowing, King of the Road again. It hadn't been the dope I had been worried about them finding, though. Because that detour to Soho in the early evening had not been simply a trip to the barber's shop. In Wardour Street I had slipped through the hardboard labyrinth concealing the entrance to a sex shop and, just as I did every month, used their contact address service to pick up from the Scotsman who ran it a small packet waiting there addressed to me. Normally I simply took it away, relabelled it and posted it to the shop again, but this time I had kept it, and it was currently stashed in the plastic bag with my jacket and the beer. Inside, the Non-Doctor vibrator box it contained looked innocent enough in its way, but the three items it held would have interested the cops. All came via my friend Freddy, the now-ailing dentist: the grand in used notes; the alternative passport for me; and, last but not least, something he had picked up just after the war, working as a lance-corporal technician with the Dental Corps in the ruins of Hitler's Germany, a light 7.65 Walther PP automatic pistol with a full eight-shot magazine. I'd had it off him with my old acquaintances in mind more than the present situation, but I was not about to ditch it yet.

The lift of relief, booze and speed did not last long. From then on, it was a long, winding way and I began to get really wretched, bone-tired and strung out. Even though, after Liskeard, I started to sense the feel of the wooded valley of the Fowey which the road wound through, the necessity of each fold and bend, I was too knocked out to enjoy it. The by-pass and dual carriageway after Bodmin, the long reaches of moor after that, the beginning of weird place-names, Catchfrench, Indian Queens, all went by in a kind of strained dream as I struggled to stay together until we arrived. It was five in the morning, still dark and there was little traffic. Once I moved up on an old van to overtake and in the glare of our headlights saw looking at me out of the back window the horned, impassive, golden-eyed head of a goat. For one of the great tourist routes the glimpses of the roadside I snatched were remarkably unkempt.

We played no music and barely talked now. Outside Camborne I asked if I could drive on to my friends; Deborah said sure, and would I like her to take over, but I stayed at the wheel. The road rose and fell until the long approach to Hale, and I gave a weary grin at the sign still there boasting its Three Miles of (elusive) Golden Sands. We drove along beside the estuary. We had reached the North Cornish coast now and, clattering through the town and underneath the granite arches of the railway bridge and out, in the dark the estuary lay to our right again; from there on we were crossing from the north of the West Penwith peninsula, the Atlantic side, to the south, Mounts Bay and Penzance. I was heading for the north coast eventually but I couldn't exactly remember the way through from St Ives, and, if memory served, going via Penzance was quicker.

So we climbed and swooped the last few miles down to the coast and Mounts Bay. After a roundabout we were driving beside the railway line and sidings with old-fashioned Pullman coaches converted to holiday homes. I was still on headlights but, snatching a glimpse or two left of the sea, I could make out a dark silhouette of St Michael's Mount, the island in the bay topped by a castle, against the flat pre-dawn grey. At the last moment I spotted a sign I remembered and, before we reached the grey and white town of Penzance, turned right, working my way uphill on a very narrow road through the housing estates behind the town and out up into the open fields, before turning right once more and starting the climb up and over the peninsula to the north coast and the Atlantic again.

It was a gentle gradient mostly, but uphill all the way. I remembered Denny had run out of petrol further up and free-wheeled clear back to Penzance one time. At first you could make out woods on either side; then we crested a hill and ran between hedges that rose well above head height. The rain had sluiced gravel in hillocks to the side of the road. I hurried on, over a tiny humped bridge, through a village, past granite hedges overgrown with ivy, then climbed again and beneath a folded hill swung right, drove carefully through the mud on the road before a single farm and then burst out on to the moors.

The narrow, light-coloured road seemed to be raised from the gorse and ditches and stone-walled fields around it. We went on for a mile; as the car approached the top of the moors we seemed to be driving into the lightening sky itself. Then the road levelled; in a gateway a single tall finger of granite gatepost, irregular, stood out against the slate-grey sky.

As the road began to descend, I pulled over into a muddy lay-by, put on the handbrake and switched off, and after a while unbuckled my seat-belt. In the quietness, with the car's engine finally silent, I sat looking at the view ahead and below; mouthed to myself 'Ho Thalassa,' the Greeks' greeting to the sea and gently shook Deborah awake.

'We're there, Deborah,' I said.

It was dawn. Before us there was grey sea, luminous sky, soft well-defined grey-blue clouds, and the coast. To the west, on our left hand, the coastline swelled and then dipped in an indentation down to a tiny village; it lay, square granite church tower, low modern barns, white-windowed stone houses, in deep green fields at the centre of a spidery network of stone-built walls and hedges, the fields dotted here and there with tiny blue tractors or red trailers like children's toys. Beyond the village out along the coast was a rocky headland; then inland to the right the land above the road through the village abruptly changed colour to the darker green of bracken, and a sheer shape rose, an unbroken sweep of hill climbing to a peak of grey rock, the Quoit, before running in the sheer gentle curve of a long ridge back over the moors we had just crossed. Beneath the line of the ridge, the hill's flanks were the flat brown colour of dead bracken, dotted everywhere with big grey stones. The hamlet nestled beneath the slope. Gulls wheeled over it; out to sea a single small ship hung in the grey curtain, apparently motionless. The sea and then the sky above went up, high and shining bright from the light off the water, both here and from the south coast close behind us; the place was ringed with water and light, like an island. Sea, cove, village, hill; all connected by stone and light, all one.

Deborah put her arm around my shoulder.

'You made it, then.'

Chapter 10

Deborah stroked my hair, and after a moment I leant and kissed her. Her young skin was fragrant still. Desire fought with bone-weariness, physical despair. She pushed closer, pressing herself to me, whispering, 'Jack.' Through my shirt and her sweater I felt the soft thrust of her breasts. I lay back, in a dream, looking through the windscreen at the valley below. I didn't think I could make love to her, but she was so soft and gentle. I felt her kiss my neck, her fingers unfastening the poppers of my shirt, her lips on my chest. I closed my eyes, felt her hand unfastening my belt, unzipping my jeans. I stirred slightly as her fingers found me, began to work me.

In a dream I felt her hair brush my chest, her lips closing on me below. It was warm, pleasant. I still thought I was going to be a disappointment to her. I murmured, 'Deb, I don't think, I can't —'

'Sshh,' she whispered, 'let me.' I felt her right hand beneath my back and raised myself so she could slip my underpants and jeans further down, felt the warmth of the black fur seat cover under me. I watched the soft curve of her shoulders, the bobbing of her head; my hands stroked her hair, then fastened on the steering wheel; I gripped the wheel tighter as her right hand squeezed me, stroking gently and steadily as her mouth and tongue went on working. I found I was getting hard; still I thought nothing would happen, but it was easier to sit still until poor Deborah tired.

Thoughts wandered through my head, light, inconsequent; how I hoped no one would come along the lonely road and interrupt us, how the sun was coming behind the hill and how fast Denny used to ride on that road down there, how recently I'd been with Sheila — a warm thought, that, somehow not incongruous with what was going on now — and how the

95

green land below abided. After an indeterminate while, to my surprise, I was very hard, and I found glowing waves were sweeping my belly and groin, gently at first, under Deborah's patient ministrations. The seat cover's fur was warm and soft beneath me, Deborah's mouth hot and wet, the only sounds the blood ringing in my ears, her sucking and the faint mew of gulls. At some moment I realized the impossible was happening; my neck felt gorged and stiffening, my stomach tingled with mounting waves of excitement and as the strokes of her hands and lips became gently more insistent I found myself groaning and gripping the wheel tighter and tighter. My eyes rolled shut, my balls tightened as an unmistakable nearly final wave came, my buttocks half lifted from the seat cover and then I cried out half despairingly as out of all my control the flood broke and soft spasms convulsed me there again and again.

Only when I had done and fallen back into the seat did Deborah remove her mouth, give me a sweet smile and a gurgling chuckle and slipped out of her side of the car. I found some tissues in the glove compartment, cleaned up slowly and was pulling on my pants and jeans as she got back in.

'Sorry. I don't like to swallow it,' she explained and gave me a salty kiss.

'You're really wonderful,' I said. 'Can I do anything —'

'Next time, when you've got your strength back,' she smiled. 'Here, come outside and smell the sea.'

She slipped from the car again and slowly I joined her. The muddy lay-by was ringed by dead brambles and there was a rusting, holed milk-churn in the hedge with bright green wild garlic growing around it; gorse straggled beyond, telegraph poles, the sound of the wind and the faint gulls' cry. In the field on the other side there was movement and black and white calves, curious and then alarmed by our appearance, stumbled and slipped in the mud back to their mother. There was a whinny and in a field further down we saw a pair of unkempt dapple-grey ponies with muddy legs canter away together down the hill.

I glanced at the car, its sides splattered all over with red-orange West Country mud. And then was jerked up short by the sight of the nearside rear wing, which was a scraped and crumpled mess. Some bastard ... And then I remembered Bristol, and the bump we'd had from the car that came out of the turning. Jesus, another foot and we'd have been knocked off the road.

I had sworn aloud and Deborah turned to look. It took five minutes and a lot of repeating that 'the driver pays' to get her to accept money to put the damage right.

Then after a minute she asked, 'Where do your friends live?' I pointed beyond the village.

'About half a mile over that way. There's three or four houses there, but you can hardly see them.' The land dipped, and the stone of the buildings was the same as that of the walls that converged there.

'I'd ask you in,' I went on, 'but they don't even know I'm coming, and it's been a while. The best thing is if you go home now and we meet up here again, same time tomorrow, and drive back together.' The words came glibly, and she nodded happily. I realized that I'd successfully arranged another leg in the trip I felt I had to make, keeping off public transport.

She was saying, 'It's so beautiful here, I only came once before —' when I made myself speak and interrupted, 'Deb, there's something I should tell you, something I should have said before —'

'You're in trouble,' she completed for me, conversationally.

'How the hell did you know?'

'Well, the fuzz rang the office, something about the van, on Thursday. Is that it?' she grinned. 'Or is it about those cold tablets that you're so fond of?'

Nice one, I thought, but said, 'No, it's heavier than that. I should have told you – if you'd been picked up with me it might have gone badly. I can't explain but I thought I'd better tell you something.'

97

'Jack,' she said slowly, 'I've always known you had nasty in you, but I've always liked you anyhow. I knew it when I came away with you last night. This doesn't make any difference. I'll be here tomorrow; if you're not waiting I'll understand. Just try and get in touch with me at the office. OK?'

I nodded dumbly, and she went round the car and got in, handed up my bag and then lifted her face for a last kiss before driving away down the hill without another word. I stood watching the little car appearing and disappearing along the winding coast road to St Ives. I felt very good, almost buoyant, again. Women can be great sometimes. Then I shivered, pulled on my jacket, turned up the collar, and breathing deep began to tramp downhill towards Trecarrick.

Chapter 11

I walked through the silent village and along the coast road, and after a mile took a footpath to the left and followed a winding track down through the fields in the direction of the cliffs. In five minutes I was standing in the silence at the end of the track outside the narrow stone porch of a low cottage, flanked by granite barns. I stood there for a long while. Then a dog began to bark and forced me forward to bang on the door. I knew if the law were watching it was too late by now, but that was not what had delayed me.

After a long while there were footsteps and the door opened. A pale plump woman in an old flannel dressing-gown, with an oval face, a tiny *retroussé* nose and long black hair shouted once over her shoulder at the dog and then stood staring short-sightedly out. I cleared my throat and started to say something when she shrieked, '*Good God*! It's Jack!'

She'd recognized me right off; I had always been clean-shaven in the old days. She was saying, 'It's been, what . . .'

'Over eight years,' I completed. 'Alice, is he here?'

'No, he's off on a course at Camborne Tech this weekend. He stays with friends over there.' At that moment a tiny straw-haired figure insinuated itself between the door-jamb and Alice's legs, and clung to the skirts of her dressing-gown, deep blue eyes staring up at me with unwavering concentration.

'Denny is doing a course at Camborne Tech?' I said incredulously.

'Denny . . .' Her oval face changed, hardened for an instant, and then she explained. 'No, not Denny – I meant Neil, the guy I live with now. I haven't seen Denny for over two years. Did you think he was here or something?'

'I don't know . . .' It had all been for nothing. I felt my shoulders sag and tried to grin. 'I was just . . . passin' through.

99

I've been up all night, you know, we drove down non-stop . . .'

'Still the same Jack,' she said and then smiled dazzlingly, and was indeed still the same Alice, Denny's old girlfriend and the mother of his child. Stooping she scooped up the little girl in her arms and held her up saying, 'Tamsin, say hello to your Uncle Jack.'

The kid stared at me solemnly for a moment, then hid her face in her mother's neck. Alice laughed and said, 'Well, you'd better come in, Jack. But I'm afraid you won't get much looking at.'

After tea and bacon sandwiches round the Aga in the low kitchen they put me to bed on the sofa in the front room. I crawled into a sleeping bag and tried for my first sleep in well over forty-eight hours. But it wouldn't come. I hurt all over, the skin of my face ached and my gums tingled from the drug, and mentally I was afraid of formless fears and spiralling deep depression. I lay there, nerves kicking and banging like cylinders firing uneven, too tired to sleep. When I closed my eyes I saw the road.

I saw once again the scene when the bomb had gone off; the horror, and Denny's figure streaking away from it. What the hell was he up to? The Basques, the Irish, what had that got to do with us, with him? And yet I knew. I remembered sitting in that very room talking with him and getting an exhilarated right-on sense of history, politics, what things were really all about; how well he expressed feelings about the injustice, hypocrisy, the subtle and not-so-subtle oppression of everyday life in the West; and of hope, of how things could be made better.

Was I so happy with life now, with the city life I'd seen over the last year? And did I turn my back on all that, the rebel days, just because I was older now, and the feelings were inconvenient? I squirmed helplessly in the sweat-box of the cheap nylon bag. Whatever the reason, those ideas seemed light-years away from me now; I had to strain to even remember the feelings which had been so fierce then. I called to mind the classic reactionary riposte – anyone worth his salt is a radical when he's under thirty – and a Conservative after that. Which even I could see helped to contain the radical impulse very nicely thank you, camouflaging with worldly wisdom the fundamental contempt for the impulse it contained. It was equalled only by the new version: that every radical impulse *must* end in either foreign subversion or indiscriminate terrorism of the kind I had witnessed, and was thus automatically to be condemned from the start.

But Denny evidently hadn't been scared off, and he hadn't got old. Whatever it was that had fired him then was still alive in him now. The way I was feeling, I thought I knew which of us that made the more admirable. But I realized now in my bones that, although obsessed with the past, I was cut off from the past, without a moral compass, adrift; nothing in the way I had lived and thought up to this point seemed to have equipped me for the choice I had to make, the judgement on Denny.

Had I ever been that convinced, except when he was talking, in full flight, arguing us over? Another fragment of conversation came back to me, Denny's smiling riposte to an objection I had raised to something he had been saying.

'Jack, you're such a little bourgeois.'

I groaned now. Right as usual, Den. *Laissez faire*, go with the flow, don't make waves, had always been the name of my game. And now it had left me in full flight, mental panic. The solitary adventurer I had always posed as had adventured his way into this shit.

I lay dully listening to the house reviving, the Hoover, the dog pawing at the door, the kid's chatter. Finally I decided it was mainly down to the speed, and the chemical problem needed a chemical solution; I blearily re-emerged and got two Mogadons off Alice. I lay in the orange light from the drawn curtains, feeling light spreading in fuzzy circles out from my head, each eventually warmer and more blurred. Accepting the strangeness, in a bewilderedly humorous way, before I dropped off into oblivion.

It was early afternoon when I revived; I was hungry but there wasn't much readily available to eat, and I recalled previous grumbling about slightly erratic Cornish hospitality, people's curtness, lack of ceremony and self-absorption down that way. Well, Alice had put me up with no notice; and she had warned me I wouldn't get much looking at.

They were getting ready to go for a walk along the cliff so, after quietly distributing my various possessions in the pockets of my jacket, I pulled it on and joined them. It seemed that at least half of my premise had been correct: the law had not realized that Denny had a kid down here – no one down here knew, Sheila and I had spoken of it away from her place, and the fact that he hadn't been here for some time had caused them to overlook it. But, conversely, it meant he wasn't here; I supposed I thought he might have come back if he was in trouble and needed a safe place, but it was fundamentally a more instinctive thing, looking for him where he always used to be.

It had not worked, so all there was to do now was wait until tomorrow and go back to London; which was illogical and risky, but I did want to see Sheila once more and let her know the trouble she was in, hanging out with Denny; that, and maybe something more. But now there was Deborah too. Mentally I winced and grinned; after months of barren, lonely days and nights, suddenly within two days I had got together not only with Sheila but also a great new young lady, who seemed, against all the odds, to think I was doing something right. Sheila could still sound those deep dissonant chords in me, and I knew I must see her again and set things straight – like the rest of that time, she seemed somehow realer than anything that had happened since – but when I thought of Deborah I found I was smiling.

Outside it was a bright, windy day. I rolled up the bottoms

of my jeans as Alice marshalled her little girl and Toomy, the small sandy-haired sheepdog, and in sunshine we set off down the fields behind the house, Tamsin, a tiny, frowning figure in a red jumper and wellingtons, trailing Quilty, a soft fragment of flowered pink Liberty lawn, for security.

I breathed deep and turned my face to the sun.

'Pretty choice weather for February,' I said.

'It's been like this all week; frosty nights, and then warm in the day,' Alice replied.

The wind was off the sea; and, after scrambling over a couple of stone hedges and winding through some gorse where Toomy busily investigated the presence of rabbit, we came out on to the side of a gully at the bottom of which a stream ran down to the cliff-top; beyond the end of it lay the glittering sea. We walked along the side of the headland towards the path along the top of the cliffs, the murmur of the sea turning to a heavy roar as we approached the edge.

The tide was halfway in; the sun was over the headland by the village to the west, big breakers were sweeping in towards the rocks, and the sunlight was striking through the waves' foaming crests as they rolled towards the cliff, turning the curling peaks of the breakers silver before they crashed and broke on the jumbled rocks below in massive explosions, slow motion, of pure white spray.

To the right a wide bay stretched away east to St Ives; closer to us that way the next headland rose, the tops of the cliffs yellow with lichen, and dotted with the birds which wheeled over the sea, big white gulls and fulmars, and black rooks. The cliffs beneath fell dark, almost black until the white fringe of breakers at their base.

I turned round slowly, moving my eyes from the sea below to the curved horizons of the hills behind, and then to the high shining sky. After a while I said, 'I'd like to paint this, but I could never get a handle on it. It's too much, too perfect; like Switzerland or something. But that's not really true.'

I shrugged, unable to express it as Alice said, 'Not in the winter, boy.'

We turned left then and walked on down the path in the direction of the village, Alice pointing out things I'd forgotten, a blow-hole in the rocks below, a seal's head bobbing sleek in the water, and a beach which was made up solely of huge jumbled boulders like a fly's view of a sugar bowl, the vast rocks reddish and oil-stained. Then we came to a section of cliff where the gorse had been burnt back savagely above the path.

'The Kervises were always like that,' said Alice. 'They love to see a fire.'

'Your sister Betty's husband?' I said. 'I thought he was a social worker.'

'He still is. No, it's not Porky, it's his brothers.' And she launched into an account of all the developments at Trecarrick which I had missed in the intervening years: how her father had died and her brother-in-law's family had moved into the main farm among the complex of farmhouses and barns which made up Trecarrick; who had married whom, which couples had produced babies (all of them, several times, as far as I could follow it) and how the balance of power sat at present. This was riveting stuff, better than any soap opera. The path along the cliff rose and fell and I ambled slowly along in the sun absorbing the biblical complications of the saga as best I could, stopping only when Alice spotted some wild violets, the first of the year, and Tamsin laboriously gathered a tiny posy.

A little further on we reached a crevice in the hillside, an old shaft with two foot of water in the bottom.

'This is where we turn off for Trecarrick,' said Alice. 'Do you want to come and have a cup of tea with Porky and Bett?'

I nodded, but when I saw the crevice I remembered something. She once before had told us, laughing, how Denny and she in the summer in the old days used to make love on the cliffs below there and afterwards lie naked and wave to the fishing boats out to sea.

The old days again. I turned to her and said, 'Speaking of old acquaintance, you haven't heard from Denny at all, have you?'

Once again there was that hardening of her face before she turned to her daughter and said, 'Tamsin, Toomy's gone ahead; run after him, now.'

The little figure, trailing Quilty, stumped off sturdily up the slope through the gorse. Alice turned to me, her eyes burning, and said quietly, 'Four years ago, when she was born, he did nothing. When he knew I was pregnant he wanted me to get rid of it; when I wouldn't, he didn't visit after that, didn't write, didn't send anything, nothing. Can you imagine just what it's been like for me here; with my sister married and happy, and all the rest of them? I tried to tell him; he came, the first time when Tamsin was about six months, he was on his way back from Ireland, I think. He said he was sorry but he couldn't help all that, it *wasn't his reality*, it was theirs.'

I nodded helplessly. It flooded back now. It had always been a source of uneasiness about him; that pride, that contempt. Convention, possessions, relationships, he wouldn't be stopped or slowed by any of it: it was grand sometimes, but there had been something almost childish, wilful about it, the way he didn't consider the 'real' world worth bothering with; because, as Alice said, he thought it was 'their' reality, not his.

'He came again,' she went on, bitterly now, 'two years ago. It was nearly Christmas. I wasn't yet with Neil. Denny was up about something, he didn't say, but I think he'd been in Ireland again. He brought me a bottle of whiskey, Powers. I told him I didn't want it; I wanted money, to give his daughter a proper Christmas. He hesitated a little, then got out £50 and gave it to me. I let him think I was going to take it and then I told him no; I didn't want his money and, if Tamsin knew who it was from, she wouldn't want it either. He left after that, and I haven't seen him since. Shall I tell you what made me happy, Jack,' she went on, 'happiest of all? He's changed, he looks different now; all the shit he's done is turning up in his face. And I'm glad.'

We were looking away from each other, down at the waves below. After a while I said, 'I still think of him as my friend.'

'Yes,' said Alice calmly, 'it was always you and him. Why, Jack? Tell me, remind me. What was it about him?'

I shrugged again, remembering what I'd just thought and tried to turn it to something favourable.

'He was in charge of his accessories, instead of vice versa like me,' I said. 'And, at bottom, through all the changes he hung on to something, something he believed in: hatred and contempt for a system he thought was unjust.'

'You call this just,' Alice cut in coldly, 'the way he treated me?'

I stopped, shrugged again, and then concluded, 'And then there was the fun.'

'Yes,' she said. 'Where has it all gone?'

Tamsin reappeared from the gorse with Toomy at her heels, and we turned and followed them up towards Trecarrick without another word; until Alice in a lighter tone said over her shoulder, 'What about Sheila? Have you seen her since you've been back?'

'A couple of times. She's OK. Teaches and makes jewellery,' I said. The little lie put a shadow on our exchange and I walked on up the fields in silence. As we approached the back of the low buildings at Trecarrick I was thinking of what we'd said; and that if I'd driven all this way to find Denny, at least in one sense, I had done so.

Chapter 12

We walked up the track between the houses and barns at Trecarrick which were scattered up the hill, the main farm on the left and on the other side of the path, the old stone barn where Denny and I had slept when we'd come down for Betty's wedding. I remembered it well; it had been a big country wedding, quite a business. It was in the summer, June, and the room in her parents' farm had been full of flowers in Cornish and Italian pottery vases; and behind the kitchen door there had been a list about two and a half feet long counting down the days and all the things to be done till the wedding day itself. Porky had appeared three hours before the ceremony in shades and beads, with a freshly used surfboard on top of his van; confronted with a long list of things still to do his only answer had been, 'Well, I've done two.'

Denny, Sheila and I had kept out of the way in the barn, tinkering with the bikes, or sitting in the sun at the top of the big curved stone steps, looking out over the fields to the sea, smoking, drinking cider and playing cassettes. From the main house voices would drift over as people busied themselves with unlikely pursuits like dipping their tights in tea or rebuking their children – 'Lucy, what are you doing with those flowers? You may eat them if you must, but don't stick them . . .' Denny had come without a suit, and I remembered him appearing for the first time in the one he had had to borrow off a Kervis cousin, holding up his arms, his long fair hair falling in his blue eyes, and asking sorrowfully, 'Who'm I going to borrow my soul from?' After early mist the weather had been beautiful, the couple handsome and happy and after the wedding itself there had been dancing all night in the big barn. Not unusually, Sheila and I had quarrelled, and I ended up on my own watching Denny and Alice, radiant, dancing. As she said, where had it all gone?

Now we walked on. A stream ran from a stone spout into a square trough and then diagonally across the track; as Alice paddled in it, several of Toomy's relations appeared in a pack and began to inspect us and him, with loud comments. Beside the track, ducks slapped their webs and arched their necks forward and back like exotic dancers; an enraged and very pompous rooster, plumes and wattle shaking, raised one claw deliberately, crowed, and stepped on the nearest hen. We walked up to Betty's house. Like everyone else in Cornwall they took in bed-and-breakfast people in the summer and, by the side of the track, for the outlanders' benefit, there was a sign reading:

BEWARE
SLOW
CHILDREN

underneath which someone had scrawled 'and Porky'.

We walked past their garage and I noticed with approval a ratty old yellow Triumph 500 twin propped against the wall in a pool of oil; there was a helmet hanging on the bars, so evidently it was a runner. Then the front door of the cottage opened and a hoard of children, cousins, engulfed Tamsin. A bearded man, rake-thin, leaned on the granite door-jamb.

'Hello, Porky,' said Alice. 'You remember Jack?'

He stared for a moment and then a slow almost crafty smile spread over Porky Kervis's face.

'Hello, boy. You all right?'

'Fine,' I said, 'just passing through. That your old nail out in the garage, the Triumph?'

Porky smiled regretfully and acknowledged it.

'Bett's fetching the milk,' he said. 'Come on in and have a cup of tea.'

I looked at my watch; it was nearly four. 'I will in a bit, but I thought I'd walk up to the Quoit first,' I said, pointing out the hill on the other side of the coast road that rose protectively above Trecarrick. 'And listen, you going to the pub tonight?'

Porky nodded. 'If the babysitter doesn't drop dead first.'

'See you later then.' But, instead of climbing the hill, I turned right on the road and walked in towards the village until I reached the call-box I had passed on the way to Alice's. In stark contrast to city practice, it was clean and it worked. I dialled the number of Sheila's friend and employer, Stephen. Sheila's soft voice answered.

'Hi,' I said, 'it's me.'

'Oh, hello, Jack,' she said. 'It's nice to hear from you. I'm here all alone, minding the store.'

'Good,' I said. 'Now listen up, I've only got the time to say things once. Our mutual friend is in bother. Not on account of me; but certain parties already know about him being where I saw him. I've had to leave town. I'm at Alice's, no, don't say where, you know she lives the same place as before. Now are you going to see our friend?'

'He said he might be around tomorrow evening,' she said carefully, stiffly.

'I'm not talking personally now, but I wouldn't see him if I was you.'

'I have to,' she said. There was really no reply to that so I just said what came into my head.

'I'll try to be there.'

'All right,' said Sheila and then the pips went and I hung up. I was walking away from the box before I remembered that I hadn't warned Sheila that her place was bugged. I ran back and called again, but the phone at Stephen's just rang and rang. She must have left immediately.

I don't know what I intended to do if the three of us met; telling her what Denny was into, hearing what he had to say or warning him or both of them how much the police had found out. But I knew I had to see them at least once more before I tried to leave the country again. If the law was watching her place as well as listening, there could be some problems. But for tonight I preferred to forget all about all that, act like it was the old days and go drinking with the folks from Trecarrick. I kicked a stone and set out back towards the farm.

I suppose it was because I was so tired that the booze hit the spot so thoroughly. The pub they favoured was an isolated one, further along the coast towards Land's End. The landlord was an irascible ex-Marine commando with a heart of gold, a liver of case-hardened steel and an outsize and fiercely ravaged deep purple nose. Since nearly everyone of his twenty or so customers came from in or around Trecarrick he had to keep some sort of check on his temper, but as the evening wore on this vestigial control became more and more frayed.

He had the television on when we arrived, watching the news. Waiting for the drinks to come I was looking up at it idly; and then snapped to full attention as suddenly the images were familiar – they were re-running the picture of the Old Bailey, minutes after the explosion. I strained to hear; it seemed that an Irish group, the INLA, had definitely claimed responsibility for the bomb. There was nothing about Denny, nothing about me; Kayler was playing the same game still. But I turned away, sickened, the illusion of escaping gone.

Alice wasn't with us; she had no babysitter and said she didn't mind staying in and watching television. Away from her, Porky and his pretty wife asked about Denny. I just said I'd been away and hadn't seen him, and in turn asked about Alice's new fellow, who from what they said sounded typically Cornish; by which I mean not the natives or the landscape, but that familiar mixture of creative and self-indulgently abandoned folk from outside, with the balance usually tipped in the direction of spoiled, and who encourage each other that way.

'You're lucky he was away, boy. You wouldn't have got in to see her if he was at home,' said Porky. 'He never met Denny but he don't like him. He don't like anyone she had anything to do with before him, including all of us.'

'Bad hombre, uh?'

'More stupid, really. More than once Alice has run over to us with Tamsin and he'll be on the phone saying he's coming after her with his shotgun, but you can't take him seriously.'

'I don't know,' said Betty. 'He scares me sometimes. He helped Uncle Billy when he was blasting the rocks in the fields above the road last summer, and Billy says he thinks Neil took one or two detonators and sticks of dynamite, though he couldn't be sure.'

'He's never met Denny, you say?' I asked quickly.

'No, definitely not. He's probably got some sort of *Straw Dogs* scenario in mind,' said Porky. 'Shotguns and dynamite!' he snorted. 'He's just paranoid.'

'A paranoid,' I told him, 'is simply a person who has some idea what is going on,' and drained my Special Brew. 'Drink up, you guys, I'm getting ahead. Was your Uncle Billy the one Denny ran the French number on that time?'

'That's right!' cried Betty. 'I'd forgotten.'

It had been in the same pub, the night before the wedding. Uncle Billy, a short, grey, lantern-jawed old Cornish farmer, three parts drunk that night, had never met Denny; and, eyeing his fisherman's sweater and blond good looks, muttered something about foreigners. Porky heard, winked to Denny and introduced him as a French crabber, 'lately put into St Ives, who spoke no English at all'. Uncle Billy consequently felt he could speak, or mutter, freely and told Porky straight out that he didn't trust they buggers, boy, he'd known 'em in the war. Denny played his crabber's role to perfection, drinking nothing but Pernod and doing a lot of eloquent shrugging. It was raining outside, and later in the evening Porky suggested that they offer the stranger a lift home in Billy's car, but the old man would have none of it; having drunk a good deal more, he was now under the impression that the Frenchman, like all of them, was an Onion Johnny, and told Porky 'to let the bugger ride home on his bicycle'. But he'd finally come around, and loftily invited the foreigner to leave his Pernod

111

and 'try some of our whisky'. I never heard what happened when he found out that Denny was English.

We laughed about it again and drank up, and that is really the last coherent memory I have of the evening. I ended up asleep standing up, with my chin in my hand and my elbow on the granite mantelpiece of the open fire; and woke to find the landlord's face inches from mine bellowing, 'Go home, you bugger, go home!' as all around people fell about laughing. I couldn't move, and was transfixed by the details, close to, of the cartography of his slab-sided purple hooter. I waved away his threats and entreaties gently and, though it was after midnight, soon someone persuaded him to serve another round and the party went on for a while.

Eventually we were dispersing noisily under the stars. It was another clear night, iron cold, the sky bright, the wind up and somewhere over the fields beyond, the sea surging. I reeled around looking up at the starry sky for a while until Porky and Bett persuaded me into their motor and drove me to the top of Alice's lane, pushed me out there, waved and hooted, and drove the short distance back to turn down to Trecarrick. I lurched down the lane, feeling great, vaguely registered an old Morris Traveller parked on the track that I didn't remember from before, but pressed on straight for the front door and tried to get inside.

Except I couldn't, because the door was bolted. I made faces of bafflement under the half-moon for a while, then knocked on the door with my knuckles. Nothing happened, and I'd just raised my hand to knock again when an upstairs window flew open and a head appeared. It said, precisely, 'I'm sorry, you'll have to go away. You can't sleep here.'

It took a little while to sink in that this was the dreaded Neil, the paranoid android, back home early from his course at the Tech and exercising his rights. I was stammering, 'Hey, man, all I want to do is crash for the night, I'll be gone —' but he cut me off with that same cold, deliberate manner which was somehow more off-putting than shouting in anger.

'I'm sorry, you can't stay. Go away,' and with that the window closed with a click.

I remembered about his shotgun. I even remembered the story about the dynamite. I backed away from the house and stood shuffling my feet and shaking my head. It wasn't fair, no way. It was half a mile over the fields to Trecarrick and Porky's place and more like a mile by the road; it was also very cold indeed and I felt about drunk enough to pass out there and then. I was heaving a big sigh of self-pity when I became aware of a sibilant whisper coming from the downstairs window. I lurched over and heard Alice whisper, 'Jack, I'm sorry. Take this.' And she handed out the sleeping bag. 'Sleep in the barn. I'm sorry about him. I must go.'

'Thanks, Alice,' I said. 'I'll see you some time,' as the window closed hurriedly. This seemed more possible. I weaved my way across to the barn, which stood at right angles to the house, and stumbled into the inky interior. But there was no comforting straw or hay, just a plain floor of packed dirt and some formless shapes in the corner which I wasn't about to investigate. I considered going up the outside steps to the portion above, but at that moment there was a scampering noise from up there followed by a loud thump and a scree of nails skidding on the wooden floorboards, as a heavy body jumped down from the eaves. I stood petrified; I hate rats.

Eventually I unrolled the bag on the dirt floor next to the double doors downstairs. It was uncomfortable and draughty, but there was some light from outside and it seemed the spot least likely to attract rodents. I was already wearing all my clothes including the shirt and tracksuit top, and all I removed, laboriously, were my boots. I clambered into the bag and lay shivering with cold and apprehension, my head and nose freezing, my hips digging into the hard floor. Listening to the scampering and scuffling above, I felt about as happy as a claustrophobe under a car-wash. Mercifully, the booze shortly stunned me into oblivion.

I jerked awake to the sound of a dog barking and loud voices close by shouting my name. The shock of it cut through my initial grogginess like a bolt of electricity; I was out of the bag and fumbling for my boots before my eyes were fully open. There was the sound of a door being hammered and the voices came again, less than twenty-five yards away, from the front door of the cottage.

'Jack Hallam! We know you're in there. This is the police. Come out at once.'

As a shouted reply came, I had time to realize that the 'police' had an Irish accent. I was moving towards the door when the same cold voice I had heard earlier shouted back, 'He isn't here; I sent him away earlier. You're frightening our child. Show me some identification or go away.'

By now I was crouched by the barn door, my hand on the pistol in my pocket; in the moonlight I could make out two figures close to the front porch, looking up at the upstairs window. The second one shouted, 'If you don't open up, you'll be liable to prosecution for obstruction —' but the cold voice from above, though shaking now, cut in, 'Our phone is dead; it was working earlier. I believe you've cut the wires. Go away or there'll be —'

But his statement of intention was never completed. There came a flat roar of a pistol shot and a splintering of wood, then pandemonium: breaking glass, a child's cries, two more pistol shots into the door and then from above the boom of Neil's shotgun.

It was now or never. I ran from the barn, angling behind the house, registering a stab of agony in my ankle as I tripped on a piece of farm machinery at the same time as a shout from the front, 'Who's that?' and pounding feet on the path around the house. I scrambled over the wall at the back and set off running across the dark field towards the cliff, the way we'd walked that afternoon. My feet rustled and slipped in the hoar-frosted grass; I felt very exposed in the open field of the bright night and didn't dare look back to see if anyone was following as more

114

shots banged out.

I'd run about halfway across the first field, panting for breath, when, from beyond, the night was rent by light and sound; I fell forward heavily, covering my head as the flash from the explosion faded, squirming round to look back I saw the flames flickering beyond the cottage and heard the crackle of a vehicle burning on the track. The story about Neil and the dynamite seemed to have been true.

Then in the firelight I saw a figure standing on the wall where I had crossed it; he was looking back up the track, but as I watched he turned again in my direction. I levered myself up and ran on over the fields towards the cliff, ducking and wincing twice as shots banged out behind.

When I reached the gorse I plunged straight in and some way on dropped to one knee, sucking in painful ragged breaths, fighting the impulse to lie flat and still, to grovel into the cold earth. But whether the guy was still following me or not, I knew, through the booze, terror and disorientation, that the imperative was to get away.

I went the way we had that afternoon; after some crashing around in the gorse I found the coast path and, slipping and sliding, went along it to the left. From below, the spectral sea surged and pounded, a version in negative of the afternoon's splendour. I jogged and slipped along on the icy mud slope of the track, plumes of breath rising in front of my face. I was muttering to myself.

'This is a trip, man, a fucking trip.'

But I ran on, trying to make myself think. Whoever the visitors had been, Neil's spectacular retort could get people running from Trecarrick, and then the police. They would find out I'd been around. I had to get away. Long minutes passed, as I jogged and stumbled and then just in time I made out the crevice beside the track and turned up towards Trecarrick.

I approached the farm cautiously over the field. There were lights on in every dwelling and dogs barking raggedly. I clambered over the wall at the back and trudged steadily up the track. Suddenly a figure came hurriedly out from the main building; but he turned the other way and trotted off through the yard towards the field and Alice's place. I looked around and then broke into a jog up the hill until I reached Porky's garage.

The Triumph was unlocked and the keys were in the ignition; I shook it once and heard petrol sloshing in the tank. All I had was Porky's word that it ran, but it would have to do. I could probably have found a car there with keys in it, but that would have been quickly missed and more easily spotted wherever I abandoned it. So, taking a deep breath, I wheeled the bike backwards out of the garage and then turning it uphill, took the weight and began to push it up the stony, rutted track towards the road.

About two-thirds of the way to the top, my lungs burning and legs trembling with exhaustion, I looked up for a moment to see flashing blue lights coming fast along the coast road from the left, the direction of St Ives. I froze, then fumbled to prepare the bike for a bump-start downhill. The flashing lights, coming very fast, drew nearer; then at the last moment turned fast down the next track, towards Alice's, where a fire still flickered on the track. I pushed frantically on up the hill, trying for a jogging pace, sweating freely in spite of the cold.

At last at the top, I heaved the bike up, turned into the road and towards the village, pulled on Porky's tight-fitting crash-helmet and jumped on. With my hands on the familiar controls the thing was transformed from dead metal to righteous transportation. I pulled back my sleeve and looked at my watch to find it was half past three. Then realized another blue lamp was coming up behind me from St Ives, and I started paddling the bike along with my feet frantically until the road steepened and I let the Triumph roll down towards the village, bending to switch on the petrol and flood the carb. After a long moment trying to remember if second gear would be up or down, I chose the former, pulled in the clutch, clonked into gear and, as the bike whirred and clicked down the silent road, switched on the ignition and let out the clutch.

The back wheel locked solid so I pulled the clutch in once more and gathered more momentum then tried again. It fired raggedly, faded, then fired again; the village and the bottom of the slope were coming up just as it decided to catch and, jerking forward, staggered, spitting and coughing, up the next rise. When I switched on the lights it faltered again; but then recovered, and we were rolling.

Chapter 13

It was not the pleasantest ride of my life. By the time I had retraced our route to Penzance my ungloved hands had lost all feeling. Behind the added complication of sunglasses, my eyes were bleary and streaming and my nose running steadily, spattering back on to the shades. My knees, legs and feet, sopping already from the run through the fields, were turning into chunks of ice. But, despite the cold, I still broke out in sweat from time to time, due to the bike. It was an early unit model from the times before Triumph sorted out the handling and, as its bald tyres lurched and skipped across the full width of the winding lanes, I had vivid recollections of watching a vintage race at Brands and actually *seeing* the back of a 500's frame whipping, the wheel going out of line quite perceptibly; this was the one with the frame they had called Instant Whip. But knowing they all did it was no consolation; it was a heart-stopping contrast to what I had got used to with the Matchless. Then there was the headlight; little better than a small convention of glow-worms to begin with, there was also an endless moment's inky blackness between dip and high beam, and the light faded to nothing every time I stood on the rear brake and the brake-light came on, draining the battery.

I was talking to myself when I skirted Penzance again, going back towards Hayle until the Mounts Bay roundabout, where I took a different way to the one we had arrived on, the right fork for the road along the south coast to Falmouth. There was no light under the instrument clock, so I couldn't see the mileage though really I didn't want to; I didn't want to think of the hundred night miles I had to ride non-stop if I was to get to where I planned. And I wasn't about to stop to check the petrol or for anything else, as getting well clear in the first hour was my only chance. There was no reserve tap, and if I ran out I would just have to think of something else. One police car could finish it. All I could hope was that, in the dark and confusion at Trecarrick, Porky wouldn't notice his bike was gone for a while; but I knew I would if it had happened to me.

I was jerked back from these considerations on a right-hander, by the bike taking another agonizing rush towards the side of the road. With the front brake pulled back on the stop, I regained control of the skidding back end inches from the verge and, wobbling, awkwardly corrected my line as best I could; added to everything else, now I realized that the roads were icy. But above or below a certain narrow rev range the engine started to falter and miss, so that you were forced to go at its speed rather than the one the road required. Frozen fingers did not make for delicate throttle control either. Cursing and glum by turns, I plodded, lurching from crisis to crisis, on through the night towards Helston. Most of the towns seemed to have had by-passes built since the time Denny and I had streaked along this route in June sunshine; this was good in terms of keeping out of the public eye, but it led to my nearly getting lost outside Falmouth and, as I slowed to a halt and agonized, the bike threatened to die. I struck off blindly, anything to keep moving, and a little further on encountered the only feature of that part of the route which I remembered clearly, the road number, A390. I had remembered it, and the A39, because it had been such a good biking road; though recollection returned to mock me now as, sick with fear and struck through with cold, I followed its twists and curves through the night up the Peninsula. Before long I was riding dully, even the agony in my hands numb now, and the night out there reduced to a tunnel of dim light, with less reality than my chattering teeth.

It took me well over two hours to do the seventy miles from there on the A390 and then the A39, and I was riding in grey dawn light again when I finally approached the junction at Dobwalls with the A38, the road Deborah and I had driven down on. There were traffic lights, and they were changing to red as I approached. I accelerated, leaned over to corner left and suddenly felt the back end simply step out from under me, and finally I was down, skidding along the road on my back, kicking the bike away from me as it, too, slid along and bounced with a deafening metallic racket and sparks flying as iron scraped across the icy tarmac. I ended up still on my back, with the bike, engine roaring, lying about ten yards away from me. There was nothing on the road, and nobody came. I lay there for a while; it was the strangest moment. Then I hobbled up to the bike and switched off, noticing as I did so that I had come to rest, appropriately, midway between a Honda dealer's on one side of the road and an undertaker's on the other.

Switching off proved to be a mistake. After I'd kicked the footrest straight and decided that the scraped silencer was about the only damage, it took a lot of painful kicking to get it going again. It was my left leg that had been scraped when I went down and otherwise I'd got away with nothing worse than a scuffed jacket and torn jeans; but I groaned aloud as my bruised, frozen body protested vigorously at every kick. I already knew how low the petrol had run, as I had had to lean the bike over to slop some from one side of the tank to the side with the tap. Finally the engine caught, falteringly, and I pushed off down the A38, back into Cornwall.

Soon the road was descending, winding tightly down through wooded slopes in the dawn light, and along the valley of the river Fowey. I pulled in the clutch and coasted downhill for as long as I could, then eased the bike slowly through the deserted tree-lined bends. Work had begun to desecrate the valley with a dual carriageway; I looked up to see poised above on the bank of clay huge yellow road-making machines, standing abandoned on massive black tyres, with the menace of metal toys scattered by big unruly children.

After a couple of miles the bike faltered and I knew that this was it. I could have tried to use the last momentum to ride off the road up the slope to my right, but I took the easy way and, as the engine spluttered, I bumped off to the left and trickled down the gentle incline through the trees towards the river, coming to rest shielded between trees from the road and, laying the bike down gently on its right side, stepped off. Then stood back in the silence, pulled off Porky's helmet and looked at the old yellow rat-bike lying there; after what it had put me through I couldn't love it, but at least it had got me this far.

I tottered backwards then, until my back found a tree-trunk and I slid down it, crouching on my heels, my hands stuck inside my jacket under my armpits for warmth. I began to shake. Not just from the cold, either: what had been nagging at my mind all the way now surfaced in full-blown horror. If I was running just from the police, that was bad; they could have found me down there several different ways. But I was sure the guys back at Alice's had not been police; I had seen them fire first. There was the item about the INLA on the news, and the Irish accents, and the slamming guns. That was worse. I was in bad, bad shit. But the worst of all was that the only way they could have found out where I was, and come to take out the witness to their bombing, was from the one person I had told. It had to be Sheila. Unless she had told someone she trusted; and that could only be Denny. I shook as if I was squatted on a juddering platform. Words from a movie repeated themselves senselessly in my head. My best pal, or my best gal. Either way was a killer.

After some while I heard a sound, and then stiffened as a car hissed past on the road above. I knew I couldn't stay there. I pulled myself up and, dropping Porky's helmet beside the bike, clambered up the bank again and on to the road; then turned my footsteps in the direction I had been riding, west. The light was there, but grey. The sun would be a long time coming up over the steep wooded slopes, but the temperature was rising and mist drifted up from the damp road and hung on the trees; and sometimes birds sang.

A car passed, and then another, and I pulled off my jacket despite the chill and carried it quilted side out, rolled up like a sleeping bag. The law would be looking for a motorcyclist, or

121

for the jacket itself. About a mile further on there was a bridge, where the road crossed from the north to the south side of the river, and a big pub; I found a phone box there, and stumbled into the still interior. With clumsy fingers I dialled the long number and then listened to the bell ringing in the big house I could still imagine well; a castle at the centre of a three-thousand-acre estate in Lothian. It had been nearly ten years since I'd left there last; but as the phone rang and rang again all I could do was pray that the laird, an ex-officer of the Parachute Regiment, named Teddy Sirk, was home.

PART THREE

'Nay then, come on, and take the chance of anger'
Shakespeare, *King Lear*, Act III, sc ii

Chapter 14

'I'm so sorry,' said Teddy Sirk, 'I didn't have such a thing as a pair of jeans about the place. Will these do?'

He held up a pair of khaki pants. In the cramped interior of the front of his Jaguar XJ-S I eased awkwardly out of my boots and torn jeans and pulled on the billowing canvas slacks; with my belt round the waist they would do, though the way they bagged out would have gratified the punk downstairs. Sirk's face, ruddy and moustached, broke into a grin.

'They're OK,' I said, 'but they're not jeans. I dreamed once that I died and went to heaven, and in the dream I was wearing jeans at the time.'

We were parked on Clifton Downs in the west of Bristol, overlooking the suspension bridge spanning the Avon gorge. Ever since I had rung Sirk things had been going well. I had walked the three miles down the valley to the lonely little station at Bodmin Roads, feeling curiously light, buoyant and alert, something remembered from times before, walking away from a breakdown or a wreck. Strangely, it seemed now that what I had wanted, a return to the past, had come to me in this extremity. At the station I waited for the first train east. I could have been very conspicuous but again luck was with me. As I walked towards the little station I was aware of a great commotion about the place for a Sunday morning, big limousines, cameras, even a small helicopter in the car-park, and, at the centre of it all, a celebrity, an ex-DJ who, like me, had trimmed his straw-coloured hair to the times and was making commercials for the railways. As I bought a ticket and waited, all eyes were on him and the entourage and, when the train pulled in, no one looked as I stumbled on board; they were all trying not to stare at him. As the train pulled out he blew us a kiss.

I spent the three-and-a-half-hour journey feeding my face with a big breakfast and a couple of coffees laced with a couple of miniature bottles of Scotch, and thawed out my hands and my knees, always the last things to unfreeze. Surprisingly, the train was quite crowded. After eating I went and sat in an open-plan carriage next to a bunch of naval cadets going on leave; they clustered round a big portable music centre, surprisingly restrained and well behaved, boisterously quoting CCN standing orders re behaviour on trains to each other and trying to get the attention of a pair of very young girls in black Harrington jackets and Chelsea scarves reading photo-strip romances.

It was a grey day, with shafts of silver light breaking through when we ran beside the sea; quiet music, Blondie, that crystal drawl, accompanied us through the rolling landscape. The ticket collector made me sweat the first couple of times, but the carriage was wonderfully warm and I slept most of the way, waking outside Plymouth to find the train creeping high above the estuary of the Tamar towards the grey tubes arching over Brunel's railway bridge. Looking left I saw the traffic on the road bridge which Deborah and I had driven across on Friday night and gulls wheeling below over the grey water dotted with slim sailing boats and many buoys marking the channel. Close to, the huge nuts and bolts, the pillars and cables of the dark grey and light grey bridge slid by. Beyond the town I gazed at the deep red clay of the West Country earth in ploughed fields, thick, glistening; and thought of the mud on the Volkswagen, and of Deborah again, before drifting back into sleep.

It was a happy train and, by the time we'd pulled into Bristol past a high escarpment on the right side to the covered red-brick station at Temple Meads, I had chatted with the cadets and when some of them got off there I tagged along. My heart started pounding when I saw there was a copper at the barrier, but I was still carrying my rolled jacket and we went through in a bunch, talking about Dire Straits, with no apparent problem. In the station I got a taxi out to the Clifton Suspension Bridge, where I had arranged to meet Sirk. I'd phoned him around six that morning. It was just after one o'clock now but he was there when I arrived, neither car nor driver showing any signs of the three-hundred-and-fifty-odd miles they had covered in the meantime. A military man, the first thing he said as we shook hands was an approving remark about my short back and sides. With his brogues, tweed trousers, hound's-tooth Viyella shirt and V-neck oatmeal cashmere sweater, that would figure.

Why had he come? Ten years before, he and I had gone after some London heavies, me to save my skin, Sirk because they had been responsible for the death of his sister. The bad guys had all died; in the process Sirk had saved my life, but then nearly offed me himself for being too close to the drug scene that had done for his sister. If he was helping me now, it had to be because I had held very little back when I spoke to him on the phone. He already knew that terrorists, probably Irish, were involved in my present trouble. As an officer in the Paras in the early seventies, he had done two tours in Ulster, and was in some senses the British establishment incarnate; he would still be at war, and he would have no doubts about taking sides in this one. Also, apart from that one nearly lethal lapse, we had got on quite well during the last go-round; I thought he quite liked me. Burly, middle-aged now, with grizzled fair hair and moustache and only a hint of the intensity I knew of him coming in a certain fixity about the stare from his blue eyes, in my present circumstances Sirk still looked good to me.

I cleaned up the cuts on my knee and hand and put on plaster from the first-aid kit from the boot of the car; and after a drink of real coffee from a big Thermos, fortified with malt whisky from a small leather and metal hip-flask, he came straight to the point.

'On the way down I did as I said I would and stopped off to phone my chum in military intelligence, a chap I used to know over there called Monty Iremonger-Watts. I told him, off the record, what you told me and he said he'd look into it; he seemed especially interested about that Irishman called McMillen, as if he knew the name already. I called him back when I arrived here. It's quite a fascinating story. But first; how much do you know about the INLA?'

'Listen, Teddy, I've been in Argentina until less than a year ago. The local paper where I was ran a big headline one time: it said, "War between Russia and China". It was only some border skirmish, but that gives you some idea of the level of news-gathering I had access to. Since then, I've mostly just listened to the radio. I know the initials and not much else. The whole Irish thing seems like a bottomless pit; it's been going on for ever.'

'That's right,' said Sirk. 'It's the longest-running guerrilla struggle in Europe, and three thousand people have died. By now the Republicans are not being trained elsewhere, they're training other people – the Basques, for instance, as you can gather from your friend's movements.'

'But Denny's not even Irish,' I said.

'Let me tell you about the INLA – the Irish National Liberation Army, incidentally,' Sirk said. 'In 1969 to 1970 the Provisional IRA split from the Officials. The latter were wanting to negotiate but the Provisionals would have none of it. They tended to be left-wing, and from the North where the Officials were from the South; and to see violence as the way to win.

'In 1974 the Irish Republican Socialist Party also split from the Officials. The INLA, some of whom had left earlier in disgust at the Officials' cease-fire policy in 1972, are their active wing; they tend to be Northern too. Initially their strength was in Coalisland and County Tyrone, and always in some parts of Belfast, but now they're in Armagh on the border also. They have strong links with other organizations.

'But like everything else in Ireland – they're Irish,' Sirk went on. 'They may think of themselves as closer to International Socialism, and like the Provos they tend to operate with other groups on the Continent, against barracks and ambassadors and so on, but they're Republicans first, they want a thirty-two-county Socialist Ireland as the Provos do. And on the ground it's all very local, very particular. The last shooting war in Belfast between the Provisionals and the Officials, in which the INLA helped the Provos, was because the Officials were getting stronger in a very specific Provisional district; I could name you an INLA block of flats, it's as particular as that, really as much to do with family as with ideology. Things change all the time, there are endless splinters – due to personality, or the side-deals people get involved in, like crime or the Provos business arrangements in Belfast, or to different levels of commitment to the violence; because people do tend to change on the violence, to become uneasy about it.

'And the INLA are violent. They're the ones that blew up Airey Neave, and they were responsible for the attacks on women prison officers in Armagh. At first the Sinn Fein claimed responsibility for that, but then retracted when a report said the weapon involved was a grenade, which the Provos didn't have. It's funny about the weapons; in fact the INLA were initially thought of as more left-wing because in Tyrone and Derry, in the country, they used Kalashnikovs; Russian guns, so they must be lefties!

'So they're smaller than the Provos and think of themselves as intellectually more leftish, hence the link with other groups. Your friend may have got involved on that basis; or it may be because, unlike the IRA, who get their arms through dealers, the INLA do their own buying and carrying. And hence sometimes get caught.' Sirk grinned. 'Their sources are mainly the States, and Beirut and Baghdad. It used to be Libya as well until 1975,' here he grinned again, 'when both the IRA and the UDA, the Protestants, went to Libya at the same time; nothing from there after that! Your friend could have fallen in with them in the Middle East. You see, there are INLA gun-buyers travelling there regularly, via Greece, doubling as affluent and respectable businessmen.

'In fact you've met one of them: Frank McMillen.'

It had crossed my mind, but it was a shock; the guy had seemed so normal, likeable even.

'But if your bloke knows that,' I said slowly, 'why haven't they busted him?'

'Because McMillen is also an informer,' Sirk said simply; 'a tout, as they say over there. It was from him that the Bomb Squad learned that your friend Dennis Lee was responsible for the explosion outside the Old Bailey.'

Something fell into place; the way the police had skated over my encounter with the Irishman. Then I thought some more and said, 'If McMillen's given them Denny, then why would the Irish be after me? All I can tell the law is what he's told them already. Or is he acting on his own hook?'

'Yes and no,' said Sirk. 'We believe he's INLA and he's probably informed on your friend on their orders. But he was only one of the contacts Dennis Lee had. You've got to remember this is a small show, very complicated and very treacherous; the left hand rarely knows what the right is doing. All it would take is a leak about you from the police —'

'Or Denny getting to hear that I was there from someone else,' I put in.

'Yes,' said Sirk, stroking his moustache and staring at the dashboard, 'or that; but, however he found out, Lee could then put people on to it, and not necessarily INLA. Since the big bomb in Birmingham in 1974 the Provos have found it increasingly difficult to use Irish Brits; but they do have sleepers, people of their own who come over here on a long-term basis and since 1977 they've been organized in very small cells, two or three men only, very hard to crack. Lee may have been put in touch with a set-up like that directly, as his back-up. In which case if he'd found out somehow that you were a potential witness, they're the boys he would put on to you.'

I grimaced and shrugged, squirming in my seat as the pistol in my jacket pocket dug into my ribs. I didn't want to talk or think about what Denny could or could not have done in relation to me, so I said, 'You're very well up on things, Teddy, considering you got out years ago.'

It was Sirk's turn to fidget.

'Most of it's common knowledge,' he said; and, then, reluctantly, 'on my second tour I was seconded to intelligence duties at Army HQ Northern Ireland, liaising with the various military intelligence types there. One tends to keep in touch.'

'Does one?' I said. 'Is that where this Ironmonger-whatsisname comes in? What's his line, anyway?'

'I can't see that you need to know that.'

'Listen, I know his name, I could always look him up in a book —'

'If you did you'd simply find him listed as a retired major,' said Sirk shortly; then seemed to come to a decision. 'No, you might as well know it all; Monty runs the SAS Group Intelligence Unit at Chelsea Barracks. A lot of SAS were Paras originally, so while I was at HQ we naturally got to know one another —'

'And just down to that, he's going to help me now? Come on, Teddy —'

'All right,' sighed Sirk, 'all right. But to understand this, you have to realize that the Northern Irish Intelligence situation is as ballsed-up and complicated as everything else to do with the bloody place. There's the Irish police themselves, the RUC: they never told us anything and, though they do liaise with them, they're hostile to the British police who, they think, lift anybody Irish or at least potentially troublesome over here and dump them back in Belfast just for the hell of it. The RUC in turn are resented by the other coppers; one reason being that they're coining it. There's lots of money available and their average age is very young, so they're doing masses of overtime.

'You've got the police here, meaning the Bomb Squad and Special Branch, who traditionally have strong links with MI5 – they're the chaps responsible for internal security and all that, run by the Home Office. You've got our lot, the army, military detectives, and the SAS who equally traditionally tend to be tied up with MI6, the foreign intelligence bods and part of the Foreign Office; they and the army had worked together in the war, and then out East, Borneo, the Yemen and so on. The two of them, MI5 and MI6, haven't always quite seen eye to eye, to put it mildly.'

'I'm beginning to smell office politics,' I interrupted. 'Frank McMillen grassed to the police, to Kayler direct, didn't he? He's their man, right?' Sirk nodded and I went on. 'But your guy is SAS – he might have a different point of view?'

'Well, yes,' Sirk admitted. 'It goes back to basics really. McMillen's INLA, hard-line; Kayler's prepared to deal with him on a one-off basis because he'll deliver the goods and they'll get the bomber and incidentally bags of glory. What deal they offer Frank in return we don't know, but you can be fairly sure it's more than just personal immunity for himself. Most probably in return for sacrificing your chum Dennis Lee, a cowboy who wasn't one of them to begin with, some of their own men will be released. And in addition to that Monty and his blokes are fairly sure Brother McMillen is thoroughly double, and still very active for the INLA. There's something big coming up and it's probably liable to happen after Kayler's caught your friend and everyone's sighing with relief.'

'What sort of thing?'

'Who knows,' Sirk sighed, 'but their last big operation over here was the bomb that killed Airey Neave, and that was at Westminster.'

There was silence, during which Sirk ran through some complicated pre-flight checks with a cigar, and I sat quiet, trying to think, rubbing a hand compulsively back and forth over my stubbled chin, feeling the nerves bouncing in my face. Finally, as the car's interior was wreathed in aromatic smoke, I said, 'There's more. Come on, Teddy, let's have it all.'

'You're really rather good at this sort of thing, aren't you, Jack?' said Sirk, with a ruefulness I didn't entirely believe in. 'There is more to it, yes. As I said, Monty and his people generally are aligned with M16 and the Foreign Office. The

FO has always favoured a political solution to the Irish problem, a negotiated solution, with the Official IRA if necessary; as I see it they're right, there are really no other options except defeat, or a holocaust and permanent partition, or the present situation continuing indefinitely. But obviously the Provos and the INLA will have none of that, it's why they split from the Official IRA originally. And in this instance we have the Bomb Squad working with one of them, and absolutely unwilling to sacrifice what they see as their valuable informant.'

'You mean if your lot want to nail McMillen, which would incidentally make the Officials not unhappy, you're going to have to get him in spite of the police?'

'Something of the sort,' said Sirk, considering the glowing tip of his cigar. 'At Chelsea Monty of course is in close liaison with Special Branch, but in this instance —'

'You want McMillen out of the way and they won't wear it. And you need me to tell you where you can find him.' The promise of that information was part of the hook I had used to get Sirk here. Now I laughed, the sound harsh in the car's interior. 'I can't understand that at all. When I met him he was living perfectly openly —'

'Things have changed, in the last month he's dropped out of sight in Saudi and he's been communicating with Kayler on the blower; they know he's over here but that's all,' said Sirk. I'd guessed as much. I wasn't about to speculate aloud on whether the phone number he had casually given me would lead to Frank when the intelligence services couldn't find him, because the promise of delivering his whereabouts was all I had to bargain with. And, besides, it was just possible; he had been stoned and drinking, and though I suspected he was nobody's fool at any time, he had no way of knowing I was going to become involved.

But there was still a puzzle. I said, 'So what's stopping you turning me over to Kayler or your SAS bogeymen; they could beat it out of me quick enough.'

'Come on, old man,' said Sirk, 'we're none of us too proud of what the Irish thing has done to us, but you can't think that after you've come to me like this I'd —'

'No,' I cut him off, 'no. I should have known it was too easy, you turning up on cue like the good fairy. What it is, is that they want you to run me; to get me to lead you to Frank McMillen. That's good, because you'll have said enough about the last go-round to let them know I probably trust you; and I'm ideal, because if anything blows loose or goes wrong I'm expendable and I can't be traced back to them.'

Sirk was shaking his head, saying, 'You've got it all wrong, Jack,' but I didn't think so. I didn't like any of this. From the start it had been steely, unyielding, light-years away from the dodgy but more flexible world of villainy that I used to know.

I would have liked to trust Sirk, but in this game there was no way I felt that I could. So I cut him off with, 'If I'm wrong, what are you doing telling me all this?'

'You're right in a sense, Jack. I would like you to help us. But in return you'll get looked after, and not in the Chicago sense either. If you want to know why I'm getting involved myself, you don't have to look any further than that bomb outside the Old Bailey. You saw it; I've seen such things before. Whatever their reasons, these are bad buggers, Jack, and I'm only sorry a friend of yours is involved.'

'You know their reasons, Teddy; you probably wouldn't be too happy if there were Irish troops patrolling Edinburgh and Aberdeen. But no, I didn't like what I saw when the bomb went off. But that's the closest I've got to the last resort of scoundrels. You know me; if I'm going to help you, it will be on my own terms,' and when Sirk nodded once, I went on, 'It will have to be just the two of us; I don't want anyone else around. I want immunity for the girl; I'm convinced she hasn't been involved. I'm not turning Denny in. I want the slate wiped clean for me with the law afterwards. And I want some going-away money.'

Sirk thought about it for a while, then said, 'Can't see any problems there, so long as the girl is really innocent. What Monty's interested in is McMillen – Lee is the police's business. How much cash did you have in mind?'

'Five thousand, up front.'

'I beg your pardon?'

'In advance.'

'Oh. Quite.'

'And can you get us some shooters?' I didn't see any reason for Sirk to know about my own weapon which, given the circumstances, I thought I'd kind of keep in reserve.

'I'll telephone and see what I can fix up,' said Sirk. There was a glint in his eye, like a hound scenting game; as far as I could judge he was definitely up for it. 'What's our first move?'

'Get me to London and turn me loose; then go somewhere where I can reach you later tonight.'

'What will you do in the meantime? Bit risky isn't it, with the police after you and so on.'

'You don't need to know,' I said. 'But until I've done it there'll be no McMillen.'

'Righto,' said Sirk, and started the car; then reached across and, opening the glove compartment, took out a battery shaver and slapped it into my hand, saying, 'You'd better use this; you'll find you feel better if you do.'

'Whatever,' I said, and started shaving as Sirk paid the toll and we rumbled over the narrow suspension bridge across the gorge and out towards the M5. As the Jaguar surged forward I couldn't tell Sirk about my real motives and feelings. The vague, spiralling meditations in my room during the time before I had seen Sheila again, the gentle tug of the months when we had been meeting as friends, had given way now to an implacable surge, a tidal race of fate and feeling. I couldn't do anything but go to her now.

Chapter 15

Sirk must have been my talisman, because as soon as we parted things started to go wrong.

He drove us at an unostentatiously high speed back along the M4 to London. It was the middle of the short Sunday afternoon and the motorway was only just beginning to crowd up with returning weekenders. After Swindon I dozed and woke up to find we were passing Heston Services again. I ate a sandwich from the packet which Sirk had brought with him but found I didn't have much appetite, as under a dull grey sky the city drew nearer again.

I told Sirk to come down off the Chiswick flyover and, at the big service station which I knew on the roundabout beneath it, ran in and bought a cheap crash-helmet, returning to the car with it boxed up and in a plastic bag. My thought was that I didn't want to risk Sirk or his chums finding Denny at Sheila's place. It was only an hour or so until evening, I would have to get there on my own and, given the certainty of some kind of police surveillance, I'd have to get in there quietly, hopefully before Denny showed up, and probably get out fast if he did so. All of which suggested only one thing. My bike. I had left it still registered in the name of the last owner and hoped the police wouldn't have tied me to it.

Sirk drove along the Marylebone Road across the top of London to King's Cross, then turned left beside the station, drove up York Way and going right and left again, into the back roads of Barnsbury. I had him stop two blocks from the square. I pulled on my shades as he told me the telephone number of his club and I wrote it on my wrist, ready to rub out if necessary. I said to start getting things together there, and that I'd call him later in the evening. And then, clutching the carrier bag, I climbed stiffly, edgily, out of the low car, turned up the collar of my jacket and hit the street.

It was getting towards dusk; the air was still and quite chilly and the streets quiet, the bot-bot of my rubber boot heels sounding quite clearly as I walked towards the square. Once I had turned the corner I pulled the helmet out of its wrappings, dumped them in someone's dustbin and carried it loose and ready in my left hand. Sirk's baggy trousers flapped unaccustomedly as I walked on, fishing in the jacket's pockets for my keys, getting the one I wanted ready in my right hand before I turned the corner again into the short road that led into my side of the square.

Still there was no one about; the neighbours' kids weren't playing in the gutter and the gentrified houses had their curtains drawn. I walked on as steadily as I could, head down but eyes flicking in every direction along the cars parked by the kerb, my guts tightening up. I didn't really expect the police to watch the house, as I reasoned they would think it was the last place I would show. But with Kayler and his merry men you never knew.

I was level with the rusting heap now, and stopped, dropping to one knee as if to tie a bootlace; which left me kneeling next to the back wheel of the Matchless. I lifted the grimy green cover up from the wheel, found the padlock and tugged it to me. Jamming the key into the lock, I snapped it open and with a noise like a harp trill pulled the heavy plastic-coated chain clear of the spindles of the back wheel. I pulled on the helmet and fastened it and then, rising, peeled the cover quickly clear off the bike and straddled it.

At that moment, somewhere to my right on the next side of the square, a car engine started up. I didn't even look. My fingers flew now over the now familiar drill: air-lever, advance/retard, petrol on, tickle the carb, find compression. About fifty yards away up the square a dark saloon was pulling out fast from the anonymous rows of parked cars. I shoved the Matchless forward off its stand, put my right foot on the kick-start, raised myself, kept the throttle clamped tight shut and without benefit of the valve-lifter gave one almighty kick.

Duf.

Duf duf duf. With agonizing slowness the individual concussions of the motor followed one another. On the fifth I chanced it and opened the throttle. The engine roared and then, as the saloon lurched forward round the square, its lights coming full on in a blinding blaze, there was no time for warming up or for anything but kicking into first gear, and hammering forward and left into the square, missing the car by a whisker as it swung round the corner and shot forward, trying to cut me off. With his nose inches from my back wheel I took the corner wide, feeling the motor howling still in first, laying it over all the way, and then cranked it on and streaked down the far side of the square and, in the first unconscious decision of many, without slowing or looking left or right, shot straight out across the normally busy road at the top end of the square and over into the narrow street running down to the lights at the crossroads with the main north–south drag, the Liverpool Road.

Parked cars flashed by on either side as I gunned it down the narrow street towards the junction, the pursuing vehicle still close behind. The lights were green until we were forty yards from them but then they started to change, and from long experience I knew there was virtually no interval before the second set changed to green. I accelerated and, gripping the bars tight, flashed through on red and with no warning slammed on the anchors and swung right into Liverpool Road, the bike heeled over and hopping bouncing around over the pitted surface of the junction, a blare of horns from cars coming off the line to the left into the side of me. I had just completed the turn when there was a slamming, shattering, tinkling concussion. I hunched my neck instinctively, changed up into third and snapped a glance behind to see the dark saloon stationary and knocked at a radical angle to the lights, a northbound car stoved into its off-side front wing.

Then I was throwing the Matchless into a left turn, working

down another narrow road towards Upper Street, meaning to make my way south to the City and then east to the Isle of Dogs. As I roared up to the Pizza Hut corner and Upper Street, I realized I had brought myself out smack opposite the cop shop there; and, sure enough, when I was halfway across Upper Street, up the side road opposite, by the petrol station, where I'd been intending to turn, came screeching a maroon Triumph 2000, headlights, blue light and siren all going. The guys who had crashed must have radioed ahead; we spotted each other at the same instant, they jerked forward and out of the side road as I snapped the throttle open and the scarlet Matchless blatted past them and accelerated away west down Upper Street towards the Angel, swinging around a bus and in a heart-stopping moment narrowly missing a gaggle of pedestrians halfway across a zebra crossing.

The siren was going and the lights blazing in my mirror. Before Islington Green I hung a right, tore up Cross Street and left into Liverpool Road again, then right and left again following a familiar cut-through across the top of Chapel Market; Penton Street went straight and Sunday-empty there, and I ran the revs screaming up in third and changed up into top for the first time, the Triumph like a leech behind, hitting eighty-five as we blurred towards the back end of a line of traffic at red lights ahead at the crossing with Pentonville Road; changed down again, braked, zipped up the outside of the line of cars, feathering the brakes, realizing traffic ahead was only crossing from the left on the right-turn filter, and, snapping one glance that way, accelerated out hard from the red light across the nose of a brake-screeching right-turning station-wagon, and made it clear across to the other side.

But it didn't do; in the mirror I caught the tail end of the Triumph's spectacular slalom across the outside of the line of traffic at the lights, which they'd overtaken on the wrong side of the road, then hard over left to squeeze through behind the tail of the station-wagon where I'd left it stalled on the crossing, and I saw the maroon police car already surging towards me again. Sports engine or no, it looked as if they could out-run me, so in a snap decision three hundred yards on I turned right suddenly and headed west, going for whatever traffic might be about in the West End to slow them down.

Together we plunged downhill towards the five-way junction and the big hotel at the back of Mount Pleasant post office. The lights were green ahead and I swung over to the right lane, making to turn right, then at the last minute reversed direction and used all three lanes to swing left with everything grounding and turned down Farringdon Road, really cranking it on up the side of the big post office area to the lights, green again, little traffic, and I changed down twice at the last moment and screamed right into tree-lined Rose-bery Avenue, rocketing down towards the wild West End with the fuzz still not very far behind. I knew by now that they were very good and very determined, and their friends were going to start showing up any minute now.

You don't drive gracefully or progressively in a situation like that, any more than you'd loop the loop in a dog fight. I just went direct and as fast as I could go, punishing engine and brakes with last-second changes, on the bends heeling over till everything was scraping, and then cranking it on immediately, feeling the tyres and suspension straining to break free and skid out from under me as the torque surged in from low down and catapulted me forward, and I swung the plot upright again to line up already for the next bend. That was how we handled the right turn from Rosebery Avenue across two sets of lights, one green, one not, and into Theobalds Road; howling past a police station there – the town seemed to be infested with them at this speed – before hanging it all out in a hard compulsory left down past Red Lion Square, lights at the end green, but changing as I used all six lanes to line up for a really hard and fast right-hander under the arches and over into High Holborn; green lights again, changing again as I shot straight across past Holborn Station, jinked left with the road, dimly aware from a single glimpse back that there were probably two lots of flashing lights behind now, and then slammed into second and zipped to the right with total precision through the artificially narrow slip-road off up into New Oxford Street.

Red lights ahead where you were supposed to turn right or left, but I ran them and had the closest shave yet, out of nowhere an ambulance coming fast up from the left and missing me by less than a foot. Ahead, the traffic was all one way, coming straight at me, but on the left there was a bus lane going my way and I took it, roaring on and hitting seventy before the end of the lane and oncoming traffic forced me to scream left and right in a tight circle around the foundations and fountain at the bottom of the massive Centrepoint building and, several seconds too early, hard right through the lights there and north on to what used to be London's unofficial drag-strip, the five northbound one-way lanes of Tottenham Court Road.

Apart from the fact that the pursuit had doubled and I was heading in the wrong direction straight for another police station, I was doing fine. I had instantly unlearned all the defensive riding and traffic sense which I'd painstakingly acquired over the years. I was not just running red lights but overtaking without thinking what the other guy would do – now it was up to him to miss me; and, though it was dusk and the cars that blurred by on either side had their lights on, I didn't, because I was more interested in making the guys behind lose me than the traffic spot me.

As I accelerated up Tottenham Court Road, I felt that moment when the roaring motor really came on the cam at around forty-five and the power came rushing on. But don't think I was carried away by the romance of seeing this lot off on British iron; I was longing for a two-stroke or a multi – instant response – because with the heavy four-stroke single I had to nurse my revs, keeping the speed up faster than I wanted to go or risk fatally losing urge; and then cope with that situation on less than adequate Matchless drum brakes. But still and all, the bike was a thoroughbred – ask it a question and it came through loud and clear every time, and the hotter and faster things got, the better it seemed to respond, feeling unburstable, and happiest working its heart out on full song. Inside by now I was cold, very cold and calculating, whirling through a metal maze of traffic and bollards at seventy and eighty miles an hour and all that was moving were my feet and fingers. Mentally I had to be several moves ahead, everything had to be connected but also spontaneous enough to instinctively grab an opportunity if it occurred. Which is what happened now. A big Kawasaki had lurched forward as I roared past him, thinking this was a street race until he caught the *son et lumière* behind and sheered off. I was going up the third lane, to the right of the iron bollards lining the middle of the road, one cop car close behind, one tearing up on my left, when in an instant I finally saw how I could do something with the bike that only the bike could do, and in a long swooping curve flung it left across the nose of the second police car and, braking and slamming down the gears as I went, just managed to squeak left off Tottenham Court Road past the green pub into Windmill Street. The first car managed to stay with me but as soon as he heeled into the street slammed on his brakes; the road was closed off by a thicket of bollards, with the underground coach park opening to the left and, ironically, the back of the police station to the right. I had swung the bike wide right and then across again, bumping it with a juddering impact up on to the empty pavement between the bollards, trickled along it, down on to the road on the other side and fast away to the T-junction with Charlotte Street, with the squeals of the police car reversing hard back into Tottenham Court Road in my ears.

I turned left down Charlotte Street and rode fast but not flat out down towards Oxford Street. At the bottom I waited obediently for agonizing seconds till the lights there changed, then crossed Oxford Street and motored down into Soho Square and at the bottom end of it straight on down Greek Street, past the lit-up signs of the cellar clubs, the sex shops and

Italian restaurants of Soho; one eye in the mirror but there was nothing, though I was constantly expecting trouble from any angle as the area is usually thick with heat. But without interference I crossed Old Compton Street, switching my own lights on before I turned left on to brightly lit Shaftesbury Avenue, waited like a good boy at the lights on Cambridge Circus under the gaze of the gingham-clad folk in publicity stills outside *Oklahoma!* and presumably of George Smiley somewhere in the circus and, slipping around the traffic circle there, swung smoothly into the northern end of Shaftesbury Avenue and rode up it to the top. There I waited for a gap and then turned hard right across the traffic, heading south again across the junction at Seven Dials and down into St Martin's Lane, slowing at a line of traffic which started by the pink neon and striped awning outside the bar there, Peppermint Park; slipped through the cars on the inside to the lights there and waited for them to change, my whole body trembling now with the aftermath of fatigue and tension.

The sound of a police siren came to my ears. I jerked round but there was nothing; then, looking right towards Leicester Square, I caught a glimpse of a striped white motor, with all the advertising going, flash over the junction and on up Charing Cross Road, away from me. The lights changed and I pulled away and took the second left, driving down towards the Strand and then turning left one street from the bottom of Covent Garden, working across east again. My intention was to get over that way, keeping off the main thoroughfares, then cross one of the bridges, and do the rest of the trip south of the river where they'd be less likely to be looking.

It went fine until I reached Bow Street. I was slipping across it towards the colonnaded walk leading to Drury Lane when I glanced left and saw, about eighty yards away and approaching, the white Rover at the same moment as he must have seen me. Lights speared on, the bubblegum machine started to revolve and the siren to hee-haw as I pulled the throttle all the way to the stop and hung on, feeling the engine gathering itself for an instant before hurling me towards the junction with Drury Lane, where I swept left without pausing and tore up the one-way street without a backward glance, accelerating hard until the turning I was looking for, where I hurled right with everything hanging out and narrowly missed a double-parked ancient Volvo saloon and some lunatics clowning around outside another posh watering-hole, the Zanzibar.

The white Rover was close behind as the road narrowed and the junction with the thoroughfare at Kingsway flashed towards me; the lights were red and I was bracing myself to run them and cross. Then I screamed, really screamed, as close, too close, dead ahead a second police car turned fast right out of Kingsway and slammed on his anchors, skidding sideways to a halt across the lights there to block me out.

I changed down and braked so abruptly that I felt the back end going as thirty, twenty, ten yards ahead the striped white sides of the car flickered towards me; then used the slide, broadsided the back end of the bike and slid through within a foot of his back bumper, my right boot footing the tarmac, the front end wobbling wildly as I struggled to hold the bucking bars to the right and regain control.

I succeeded, and accelerated away again; but I had two problems now. The first was that by the time I'd stabilized and dodged the first traffic, Kingsway was divided into two by an unbroken barrier and I was on the wrong side, heading south into the face of three lanes of northbound traffic. The second was that my original pursuer had squeezed past his colleague and was coming on after me.

The traffic ahead was blaring, flashing, brake-shrieking madness; all I did was hold to the far left lane and hoped they'd go away. At closing speeds of over a hundred I flashed towards cars that only had seconds to react, as half of them were coming up from the northbound-only tunnel which ran under the Aldwych from Waterloo Bridge. I had only seconds left if I was going to cut across to the right and avoid the yawning mouth where the road divided and the two left-hand lanes shooting cars out at me like pinballs dipped down into the curving tunnel. The police car was close behind, the traffic coming towards me on the right heavy, what I could see of the tunnel clear. I drove into the tunnel. No way could a car follow.

For the first instants there was nothing coming. I held to the left as the enclosed space amplified the booming rattle of the engine insanely and the bright neon-lit tunnel curved sharply right. My eyes were jammed wide open; I had time for one flash of thought, half intuition, half logic – anything in the oncoming outside lane where I was would be fast. I jinked right the moment before a car flashed round the corner from ahead and passed, stark open-mouthed surprise on the driver's face. Then hard left as suddenly another, a Volkswagen, was coming directly at me. It was so close that as I avoided him there was a light shock – the rear wheel had kissed his running board – but I didn't react. I had no time for anything but grimly to follow the trap of the narrow tunnel as it swung left this time and started to climb. I was just around the last corner and climbing hard when it happened. Shooting down over the ramp ahead came four headlamps; two cars coming fast and abreast.

In that split second I tucked in my elbows, stiff-armed the bars, lowered my head and went for the gap between them. There was a blaring flash of coloured metal, the brush and shock of slipstream air, and then rending, heart-stopping noise as one hit the horn and the other jerked the wheel too hard and ploughed into the wall on my left. Then I had shot through and clear of the tunnel, out into the night under the lamps on Waterloo Bridge, still in the wrong lane with immediately more lights approaching fast and full on.

The northbound and southbound lanes were divided by a pavement only; I swerved right and then ran at it, accelerating hard and jerking backwards on the bars so that the front wheel lifted and only the back one slammed into the kerb, and then we were aviating across, me struggling to keep the front wheel up until the back end landed and we slammed back to earth, skidding all over the road. I barely sorted that out; then, back on the right side of the road heading south over the bridge, snapped a glance behind.

There was nothing coming, nothing except the one thing I had been dreading all along. Swerving on to the bridge behind me from the Aldwych, the orange-striped white fairing and close-set pair of winking blue lights of a police BMW motor-cycle.

Chapter 16

I rode flat out across the bridge, wind tears streaming from under my shades, the lights of the Embankment a blur, swerving in and out of the Sunday evening traffic, never slackening speed till the wide curved bridge fell away to the roundabout by Waterloo Station, where with honking and screeching from my right I dropped the bike all the way over to the left and in a howling turn with everything scraping swept around into Stamford Street, heading east again. A glance flashed in the mirror showed that the police bike was still there, and no further behind.

The road ran parallel to but behind the Thames, the river out of sight behind developments, vacant lots and grimy commercial buildings; it was heavily pot-holed but straight. The front forks jerked and clanged, bottoming on the bumpy surface, as I accelerated to the limit. I was really on full noise, faster than I had ever pushed the bike before, with the engine roaring and the needle on the Smiths speedo flickering between ninety and the magic ton as we flew over the rutted roads; I was riding crouched over the tank with everything tucked in, but a glimpse in the mirror showed the blurred blue lights still well up behind me. As the road curved round and the junction with Blackfriar's Bridge flashed towards me, for the first time I felt the clutch of real desperation; even if I could keep this up for much longer, which I doubted, there was no way a twenty-year-old 500 cc banger was going to outrun a fully-fired BMW with 800 cc capacity in those horizontally-opposed cylinders sticking out each side of it giving a 120 mph potential, and ridden by a highly trained professional.

The lights at the Blackfriar's junction were green; we flashed across and hared on down Southwark Street, dodging round the occasional car. I didn't dare break concentration to look behind or in the mirror but I sensed him gaining on me. The road began to swing round towards Southwark Cathedral and London Bridge and I had a decision to make – follow it, and cross to the north again or along the river at Tooley Street, or cut down right into Borough High Street and south. Everything looked bad; though he couldn't report my position on his R/T without stopping, north of the water the City would be deserted, giving his speed the edge; all I had was my machine's lightness compared to his, and its lack of bulk.

Its lack of bulk.

I had been about to fling into a right turn and head south for the Elephant and Castle but at that instant, something, a memory and a decision, flashed in my head. As we passed under the first railway bridge, I slammed on the anchors and changed down once, twice, the motor screaming as I heeled left and rode up on to the pavement beneath the bridges there, accelerating along the walkway with viaduct walls on my left, and behind me the police rider who had faultlessly followed every move I made and was by now within yards of my tail. Rounding the corner two Japanese tourists in raincoats leapt for their lives as we roared on and then I braked again, swung as far right as the wire barrier allowed and then pulled left and, just as I'd done when I scored the speed with Doctor Lockyer that time, squeezed the bike trickling through the narrow bollards into the cut under the bridge beside the cathedral.

I pulled away fast to the end of the row of derelict buildings and snatched a glimpse backwards to see, as I'd hoped, the police BMW, lights still flashing, engine revving but with its protruding horizontal cylinders stuck firmly against the base of the bollards, too wide to wriggle through. From behind his goggles the moustached rider looked up to give me one impassive glare.

I didn't stay for a second look; he was already backing off as I slipped left around the corner. Now I could try and lose him in the maze of narrow streets behind the Borough Market there and head for Southwark Bridge, or I could run for it back the way we had come down Southwark Street. But as I reached the end of the narrow cut under the bridge and faced Southwark Street again, I pulled into the far left-hand side of the alley and drew to a halt, forcing myself to wait. The engine ticked over slowly with a steady quiet throb beneath me. Sure enough, in a few seconds the police bike shot into view from the left, running back fast but steady along Southwark Street, presumably intending to catch me if I came up from the back streets or, failing that, to plug up Southwark Bridge and then call for the cavalry. I waited until he was out of sight around the curved road, then revved, kicked into gear and, under the astonished eyes of the Japanese tourists who had just appeared from round the corner on the pavement next to me, shot forward, crossing over Southwark Street and cut through south into Borough High Street, heading for the Elephant. As I gunned the motor away there was time for a brief grin. The police may have called their last Triumph bikes Haemorrhoid Specials, but perhaps that business with the bollards would encourage them to buy British.

I turned off the High Street left down Great Dover Street, following the signs east for the A2, but at the big roundabout and flyover at the start of the Old Kent Road headed left again, back north; within a minute I had rattled across Tower Bridge with the Tower illuminated on the left, skirted the new hotel and St Katharine's Dock development and, following one-way signs, worked down into the road running east again through Wapping, closest to the river and the ravaged dockland; I could have cut up to Commercial Road but in this industrial waste-land there was less likelihood of heat or indeed traffic of any kind, except the occasional tourist exploring the famous river-side pubs. I throttled back and bumped along the rutted way. The scarlet Matchless with its pepper-pot silencer internals was never going to be inconspicuous transportation, but there was no sense in inviting attention.

It was full dark now and, as the road swung left through the derelict dockland, I pulled back my jacket cuff with frozen fingers and checked the time. Past six. I started to shake again. The road reached a T-junction and I turned right on to the Highway, still parallel with the river, picking up speed, trying to control my body and my dread by giving myself something to do. When the road forked I took the main branch, left up to Stepney East Station. There had been a maze of Limehouse back streets ahead which probably led through to the Isle of Dogs, but I didn't know the area and opted for a quick blast down the way I did know, the route I had taken at Christmas: turning right at the station and riding down the wide East India Dock Road, head on the swivel for the law, but there was nothing, for a few fast miles until on my right I recognized, incongruous in the rough area, the spire of a tall pillared eighteenth-century church standing on a green, and a little further on the bingo hall, a converted cinema, where I swung right and headed down the eastern side of the Isle of Dogs.

I rode past the modern blocks of flats and then the road closed in and began to twist between grimy brick walls on the right and corrugated-iron fencing on the left blanking off the river beyond. Ahead a sign painted white on the brick said, 'WELCOME TO THE ISLE OF DOGS', next to a depiction of the rough horseshoe shape of the island and a crude crane, echoing the angular silhouettes of the real things themselves, which despite the night I could make out in the sick orange glow of reflected sodium lights. I was feeling very bad, hemmed in by the narrow walled way – there was nowhere to run and I was cold meat if anyone was waiting or came up behind – and the uncertainty of what was about to go down ahead.

We clattered on, the bike's engine noise thrown back metallically by the close walls. Half a mile on, with the cranes crowding in close, I drew to a halt at traffic lights where a narrow bridge, divided by iron down the middle, crossed over the first of the channels that led into the dry docks of the Blackwall Basin off to my right behind the brick wall. It was one-way traffic only over the bridge and I waited for the lights to change, though no cars crossed towards me. The lights went green and I crossed over the bridge; on the far side there was a little road running off to the left, Coldharbour Lane, but I drove past it and straight down the main way. I was getting very close now, there was only the next bridge to go and I would be there, and the fear and tension were making my hands squeeze the grips like claws. Just a few hundred yards further on I swung slowly into the last series of bends before the bridge. And slowed even further, inside squeezing up, because up ahead I caught the blink of flashing lights.

There was no way back. Alone on the road I eased gingerly right around the last corner, stroking, then drew to a halt beside the kerb. Ahead of me red and white poles were lowered with a wire barrier dangling beneath and flashing amber lights either side, like a continental level crossing. Beyond the road rose straight into the air. They had raised the bridge.

I couldn't believe this, didn't know what was going on at all. But there were people above, in a glassed-in observation compartment like a control tower halfway up the broad right-hand pillar of the bridge, so, after a moment, noticing that Coldharbour Lane emerged as a narrow road to the left, I turned and chugged down it, past a short row of terraced houses and at the end a tiny pub. The lane went round the corner there, the buildings ended and tall corrugated-iron fencing began again. I bumped up on to the pavement and, leaning the bike against the fencing next to a gap where kids had pulled a section outwards, went to switch off, but the Matchless pre-empted me, coughing once before giving up the ghost. I switched off anyway, took off my helmet and, with a sudden thought, shook the machine. The faintest possible sloshing came from the petrol tank; I realized now that the Matchbox had faithfully carried me this far on well under half a gallon, but there were limits. I could probably get off the island on reserve, but I would think about that later. Stepping off the bike I looked around; the back street was badly lit; there were a few cars outside the houses but nothing moved and the only sound was a murmur of voices from the pub close by. I stood for a while, sniffing the river on the night air; then, putting the helmet beneath the bike, unsteadily and uneasily walked away, back towards the bridge. Something felt wrong.

I rounded the corner cautiously and looked again. Everything seemed normal. There were a couple of cars waiting by now in front of the barrier, and then the raisable bridge, modern, the stubby pillars very wide and painted a dull turquoise, with the brightly lit glassed-in control box jutting out to the right, and a big drive chain coming from each side to beyond the lights; above, the double pivoted arm with four cross-pieces, looking like an empty window frame, tilted up into the sky. It was too elaborate for just stopping someone getting in and out; and, sure enough, looking to the right along the channel into the docks, further down under the floodlights I saw a big ship sitting ready to come out into the river. Just happenstance; I had turned up at the wrong time. I could ride back to the main road and down the west of the island to approach Sheila's house from the other side of the bridge but, even if I didn't run out of petrol first, by the time I had got round probably the ship would be through and the bridge lowered. It was quiet now; with English resignation the cars had switched off their engines and sat queuing patiently. I should have done the same, but I was actually feeling physically ill from a frightening intuition that something was very wrong.

With the bridge raised, from where I was I could not see Sheila's house; I walked across the road and stood outside the high locked wire-mesh gates topped with barbed wire that gave access to the docks. Through the mesh, over the water, I could see her place, the end house of the straight tree-lined road; it was framed by the trees and at the back gave on to the towpath down to the basement. That was the way I would try

152

and get in, around the back and up the cast-iron fire escape that I had noticed running past her hot-house aviary; trusting that the law was just listening or, if watching, only around the front. It was a risk, but necessary. With a jerk I realized lights were burning in the tall top-storey window. She was there. But alone, or with Denny?

At that moment I heard the first, faint donkey-bray of sirens.

I stood paralyzed for long seconds, then started shifting from foot to foot in indecision. As far as I could tell the sirens were coming from the south, up the island from Millwall. It might be something else entirely; but whatever it was I should fade away back to the bike and get clear. But something kept me there as the sirens got louder and louder, staring helplessly at Sheila's house less than a hundred yards away across the water.

Then with absolute abruptness it happened. The night was split with blinding light. Like a speeded-up film of a flower blooming, a blossom of fire and smoke exploded from the top floor of the building and the echoing roar of a massive detonation ripped across the quiet of the docks. In slow motion, it seemed, rubble and glass cascaded down, pattering on to the road and splashing into the channel behind the house. As the overpressure of the blast reached me, I ducked, catching a glimpse of the men in the control tower on the bridge holding their ears. When I looked again, the two top floors of the house were wreathed in bright white smoke and the thin tongues of yellow and orange flames, the fire taking hold instantly, crackling and licking hungrily, illuminating the road below where police cars were skidding to a halt one after another. One more crazy noise joined the others: outside the house a black dog, maddened by the explosion, barked furiously, turning on itself.

The drivers of the queuing cars were half in, half out of their motors, staring across the channel. People had come dashing from the pub and the houses in Coldharbour Lane. I stumbled to the back of the line, stopped, stared myself; after a while I realized no one had eyes for anything but the burning house. The bridge was starting to lower as I slipped down Coldharbour Lane and reached the bike. Working like an automaton, furiously I pulled back the corrugated fence till, as the din of fire-engine bells drew nearer, the loose flap was big enough to force myself and the machine through. I left it there, leaning against the fence on the rough ground running down to the muddy banks of the river. Through the fog in my head I still knew that, with the way the police would be converging, this was no time to be riding away on a machine they were already looking for with just a thimbleful of petrol in the tank. Crawling back through the fence I regained Coldharbour Lane, and began walking quickly away down the deserted narrow street.

Chapter 17

Two hours later I sat south of the river in the public bar of a pub on Blackheath, near the village. The public bar was smarter than most of the saloon bars I was used to, and the bar staff's looks had said they weren't too sure about my boots, leather jacket and Sirk's bags. But it was a quiet Sunday evening; with only a juke box, fruit machine and the pulsing throb of a quiescent Space Invaders machine as well as one other couple on our side, they let it go. I remember being quite concerned about it; I was completely numb inside and acting mechanically, and my worry was not about attracting attention, but giving offence by being somewhere I wasn't dressed for.

There was also a telephone. I'd called the number Sirk left me and spoken to him. I told him briefly about the explosion and asked him to get in touch with his intelligence friends and find out via them from the police what had happened. He promised to do so immediately and asked where I could be contacted; I said I would ring him back in half an hour. In the meantime I made two more calls. After that I drank a Scotch sparingly; it was a difficult time to get through. After a while I got up and went over to the juke box. There was nothing I liked except a Dire Straits record: *Romeo and Juliet*. I put it on and listened.

Juliet, when we made love you used to cry
You said I love you like the stars above, I'll love you till I die.

I sat when it was over. A voice came into my head – 'I'm tired,' it said, not whining, but wistful. 'I'm so tired.' I talked to myself internally, telling the voice it wouldn't be much longer now.

Finally I looked at my watch again; it was time to call Sirk. I drank my Scotch and went to the bar for another. My body ached, bruised and weary, and frozen not with the ride so much as the wait at the bus stop, nearly an hour in a windswept gulley by the Blackwall Tunnel. From Coldharbour Lane I'd slipped half a mile north through the back streets up to the East India Dock Road again, where it bridged the tunnel approach, and walked down to the bleak cut with continuous traffic roaring by, to wait for a bus south through the tunnel, my mind and body chilled through, unable to think any further than the idea of getting clear.

I picked up my drink, walked to the phone and dialled Sirk again. They put me through to his room and I heard him say, 'I'm afraid it's bad news, Jack.'

I waited in silence, knowing already.

'They were killed, both of them; the girl and your friend.'

I stood in silence listening to the steady pulse of the Space Invaders machine like an amplified heartbeat.

'Are you all right, Jack? I'm so sorry . . .'

'I'm all right, thank you,' I said carefully. 'How can they be so sure, after a blast like that . . .'

'The tapes, Jack. They were still bugging the place. When the people listening realized it was Lee talking to the girl they immediately alerted their men. But before they could get there the place went up.'

'Who did it?' I said.

'They say it was an own goal; I'm sorry, I mean that they blew themselves up. It seems they had been quarrelling. I'm sorry, Jack . . .'

'I want to hear the tapes,' I said. 'Arrange it. Tell them to be ready to play them to me over a phone. I'll ring you back and you can give me their number to call.' As Sirk started to protest I cut him off with, 'Do it. Because I know where Frank McMillen is for sure now. And no tapes, no McMillen.' I hung up.

There was a click as they switched on and then the tape began abruptly with the sound of conversation; it must have been

156

voice activated. Sheila's melodious voice came, surprised.

'What ... Denny – how did you ... What are you doing with the wine? If you want a drink, there's some Scotch ...'

Then for the first time in so many years I heard Denny's voice again. Faintly uncertain accents wavered there as they had always done, someone trying to be more proletarian than their actual origins, but less than before; he sounded rougher, but there was still the lilt and I could see his face as he said easily, 'Sorry to make you jump. I slipped in up the back, for obvious reasons.'

'Listen, Denny; on the radio this afternoon I heard about something down in Cornwall, an attack on someone at Trecarrick. I rang Alice. She told me two men had come to their house after Jack last night, they pretended to be policemen but then they started firing pistols at the house until her boyfriend Neil saw them off. She said they sounded Irish, and the police, Special Branch she thinks, have been there asking a lot of questions. Were they Irish, Denny? Have you got mixed up with them? Yesterday you said it was all a mistake, outside the court, and that you were there watching but had nothing to do with the bomb, and I tried to believe you because I love you, no, let me go on. Jack said when he rang that no one knew he was down there. Except me, after that; and I told you. Were those gunmen your friends, Denny? Did you tell them where Jack was so they could shut him up about having seen you?'

'Do you believe that? Jesus, Sheila, you're going to pieces. You don't like it, do you, when it really comes to it – getting your hands dirty.'

'I've never found anything important enough to betray or kill my friends for, if that's what you mean.'

'You just don't hear it, do you; the soundless wailing in this God-forsaken land. I do, you know, I hear it. I am the crowd in the supermarket, I'm the kid getting his mind rotted along with his teeth, I'm the woman dragged off for shoplifting, I'm the foolish middle-aged bloke who looks confused because his dignity's gone with his wage —'

157

'You're getting off the point! I live here with the docks dying all around, and I work at Tower Hamlets. You don't have to lecture me about injustice; but I can see that some of it's equivocal, and some of it's remediable – violence isn't the only way . . .'

'Yes, and if I wait until I'm forty I'll understand everything and forgive everything. Jesus, you know what you remind me of? Once, just one time, I saw a shrink; and you know what the heart of his method was? He'd get you to dredge up your memory of the moment you found out what the world was really about, not the fairy-tales they tell you till then – the moment when oppression bit into *your* skin. He laughed and told me about a man, a company director, something, whose whole inferiority shot got down to a spanking he'd had when he was five; there was more to it than that, but that was when they got to him. Then the good doctor shows Mister Big the absurdity of it, and Mister Big is reduced to saying helplessly, "But they *did* hit me with a hairbrush." They break the poor cat's spirit from that moment on, but the doctor's laughing, he's squirting foam on that little fire which is really all the other guy's got. And finally the poor guy is laughing with the doctor, he *sees* the absurdity of it, a man of his age fretting about a spanking, a man like him. And from then on that's what he'll be: a man like him; not a man.'

'I don't understand what you're saying.'

'No you don't, do you? I'm trying to tell you that you have to keep your passion alive. Anything else they can co-opt or subvert. But not your passion. It's the only answer.'

'No; not on its own. Thought too, reason too. Not on its own, not without limits.'

'Philosophy is for before and after, baby. If you can talk like that, it's not getting to you. But with you, what does it take to do that, eh? You're living off your hump, socially; your expensive education – she's *so* well-spoken, I bet they say – your good health, but, above all, your blinkers. I guess you get them from Daddy. I hope they last you longer than his did —'

'Leave my father out of —'

'. . . Last you after the money runs out. They say truth comes in blows; I guess the car that knocked him down was a shot of truth. The great Captain Rayner with the wheelchair blues – when he wanted to sue the driver and the hospital, finding out just how much it costs for an ordinary person to go to law; no attendance allowance for you because of the cuts, so getting dependent on a young harassed social worker whose visits aren't frequent enough —'

'Shut up, Denny . . .'

I could hear Sheila was crying by then. In the pub as I listened someone was playing Space Invaders. The machine's pulsing bass beat to a faster rhythm as the noise of electronic explosions came quicker.

'. . . Getting depressed, too apathetic to go to his therapy sessions, drinking, drinking so much he starts falling out of his wheelchair, drunk, but the money for whisky's running out and the Captain can't conceive needing a drink, or anything else, and not having the cash for it, so he just carries on until all the money's gone. And then finding out there's nothing he can do about it, and winding up a cripple at the mercy of the staff in a state-run home because that's the way our great society ordains it should be, and nobody cares enough to do anything for him —'

'Shut up, you bastard! Shut up! Oh, Jesus . . . All right, all right, you know I've thought all that – I know, God knows, I haven't done everything I should. But whatever he's come to, I can still remember, remember what he was . . .'

'. . . A good bourgeois.'

'Yes! Yes, but in his own terms, upper-middle-class terms, thirties terms, he did what he could. We can't live in those terms, we have to criticize them and laugh at their absurdities, get ourselves separate; but still see them, older people, our parents, sympathetically —'

'Sympathetically? Jesus!'

'With sympathy for what they tried to be, when it was

worth while. Because that's all there is. That's the only way our children will ever —'

'Our children! There aren't going to be any, not like that —'

'. . . Understand this, that's the only way we can understand each other.'

'And do you think you understand me like that?'

'You! Always back to you!'

'Why not? You and me, that's what we're talking about now, isn't it?'

'If you want to make it a competition, go on.'

'What else is it?'

'A dance, it can be a dance. We've been so good together —'

'A dance! There's only two dances I'm interested in – the dance of death that's going on all around us, in and out of the supermarket they've made of this country. And the dance we'll do on the ashes of this shithouse when we've torn it piece from piece and burned it to the ground.'

'You may be as angry as you say you are, but who hears about it except me? Who do you make suffer for it but me, and I'm on your side anyway?'

'Ask them in Pamplona —'

'Or outside the Old Bailey. In Spain you said you were just helping people get away, across the border. But what about the Old Bailey, Denny, what about the bomb?'

'Whatever you say. You're upset. Listen, I'll just —'

'Leave that wine alone. You don't drink here, or eat here, or set foot in here again. I know you now. I know what you're doing. I know what you tried to do to Jack. I don't like you any more, Denny. Get away from here!'

'OK, but I'll take —'

'You want the wine, Frank's fucking wine? WELL, TAKE THE . . .'

'Oh Jesus, leave it!'

'. . . BLOODY WINE.'

With an abrupt click the tape ended. I was left listening to the hiss of the re-recording running on blank. In the background the game of Space Invaders was over and there was just the steady throb, the slow heartbeat of the machine at rest. She must have picked up the crate in her rage and flung it at him; and some part of what Frank McMillen had left for Denny inside it had been impact sensitive. I had a vision of Denny's face as it would have been in the moment before the crate exploded: terrified, then supplicating, then in some way confirming; and knew that she too must have realized what they had done to each other.

I replaced the receiver carefully. The landlord was calling time; it was only ten thirty, but I'd forgotten it was a Sunday. I went out, fastening my jacket, and began to walk across the broad grass expanses of the heath.

Chapter 18

The heath was empty of pedestrians and, in a darkened area away from the tall lamps, I dropped to one knee as if to do up my bootlaces; my hands trembling, I loosened them off, slipped the pistol from my jacket pocket, jacked a round into the chamber and put the safety back on. Freddy had shown me how this not only secured the piece but also tripped the knurled hammer, for the Walther was a double-action automatic; left like that, without cocking it again, it could be fired just by slipping off the safety catch and pulling the trigger. I slipped two pounds of snub-nosed pistol well down into the side of my right boot and cinched it up with the long laces; the curved heel of the eight-shot magazine protruded and I was grateful for Sirk's long trousers with their loose flapping bottoms. I straightened and walked on; until, midway across, a car parked alone flashed its lights once. I went to it and the Jaguar's door opened.

Sirk looked at me carefully as I settled in the low seat. But all he said was, 'And where would you like me to take us to?'

'Go north through the Blackwall Tunnel and then keep on north and east, up the A12 towards Great Yarmouth,' I said. 'I'll tell you when we get close to where we're heading for.' I didn't want any of his friends pre-empting us. 'But I can tell you this now,' I went on, 'it's a boat and we have to be there before dawn. Have you got a large-scale road atlas?'

Sirk handed me a navigator book as he started up and pulled away, and I checked through the index and found the pages I wanted. By he time I had roughed out a plan we had slid through the arched claustrophobic reaches of the northbound Blackwall Tunnel. On the dual carriageway running north from there I said, 'Did you get the stuff I asked for?'

Sirk gestured at a canvas grip on the floor by my feet. I

picked it up and unzipped it. Inside, wrapped in their straps of webbing were two shoulder-holsters holding heavy automatic pistols.

'They're 9mm Parabellum Brownings, the NATO pistol,' Sirk said. 'They've a thirteen-shot magazine, a high muzzle-velocity and they say the rounds are hollow-points, so they should be fair stoppers. Unfortunately they couldn't get us silencers at short notice.'

'It should be all right,' I said.

'Can you use an automatic?'

'More or less.' There were spare magazines wrapped in oilcloth, and also a flat oilcloth packet containing a manila envelope full of new banknotes. I glanced inside and then slipped it into one of my jacket pockets.

'I didn't count it,' said Sirk drily as he negotiated the Old Ford roundabout and came out from under the flyover following the signs east towards Leytonstone. Then in the flashing lights of the streetlamps passing overhead he glanced at me again and said, 'You're sure you're all right, Jack?'

'Never better,' I said, and this was not a word of a lie. After hearing the tapes, rage had come to me voluptuously, like the rush of a drug or sexual excitement; there was the same incisiveness, the same brushing away of anything irrelevant to release. I asked Sirk, 'We're going to get McMillen, right?'

'Well, yes, that's the general idea —'

'Fine,' I cut in, 'that's fine by me. I've seen a bomb rip up innocent people twice now; I've been busted, taken a kicking, been run out of town, shot at and chased up and down; the woman I really rated has been killed and an old friend, whatever he had become now, got betrayed, and it's all down to these bastards. All I want now is McMillen dead and the rest of them out of our fucking country.'

'Yes – of course, funnily enough, that's exactly what they say about us,' said Sirk and when I started to speak overrode me with, 'No, Jack, now steady. There's nothing wrong with being fighting mad, just as long as it doesn't get in the way of your

163

judgement. We made that mistake too often over there; that and underestimating them. These things are best done with a cool head, believe me.'

'All right,' I said, 'all right.' Inside I nursed the tense, somehow inflated sensation of pure anger, feeling how it made everything easy – there was no room for fatigue, or fear. But I could see the sense, tactically, in what Sirk was saying, and after we had cleared Brentwood and got on to the A12 proper, I asked him to pull over to a lay-by and, when we halted, switched on the interior light, showed him where we were going and told him how I'd found out.

'I rang the number McMillen gave me and when a guy answered I asked for him. Never heard of him, the geezer says, this is Pin Mill Hard. I couldn't say Pin Mill what, so I just described Frank – large bloke, receding hair, shades, all that, and the guy says, Oh you mean *Frank*, big Frank, yes, he's about, but they're on *Hotspur*, they took her off with the tide this afternoon. I'm beginning to get the picture, I've even placed the guy's accent as probably East Anglian, so I say, sorry, I thought I was phoning Frank's place and he says, no, he's just a guy who works at one of the boatyards there and lives close, and he didn't mind taking a message now and then for O'Connor, the bloke who owns the *Hotspur*. He said O'Connor and Frank and another guy were on board and they'd floated her off and dropped down river to Butterman's Bay that evening, so they could get out at low tide next morning. I can't very well say where is all this at, so I tell him I may want to get there to join them and just where will they be? He says all the other barges are laid up on the hard so I can't miss *Hotspur*, they'll be the only one in the bay, anchored well north of the tideway because of the ferry and the other heavy traffic up to Ipswich.

'And that's about it. On your map I've found Pin Mill, it's here, east of Ipswich on the Orwell, and I guess the hard is some kind of mooring —'

'That's right,' said Sirk, 'and it's odds on their craft is some

164

kind of sailing barge – you know, those great big ones, eighty foot long; with the ochre-brown sails; a friend of mine had one and I went out with him once or twice —'

'Christ, Teddy,' I said, 'is there anything you don't know about? Well, anyway, here's Pin Mill and here,' I jabbed a finger a couple of inches further east round the blue of the estuary, 'here's Butterman's Bay. If they're anchored north of the channel I make them somewhere around this bit of bank, below this village, Levington. If we go to Ipswich and then turn east for Felixstowe, turn off the main road down to Levington and leave the motor in the village, it's less than a mile's walk to the shore. If their's is the only big barge out there, we should be able to suss it.'

'And when we do,' said Sirk, 'how do we get out to it?'

'It's a river bank, right? There'll be boats.'

'Yes, but in the middle of the night, how do we hire   ? Oh dear,' said Sirk, shaking his head as he caught my drift, and started the car.

'Listen, Teddy, I'm starving,' I said. 'Are there any more sandwiches?'

'One or two, I think,' said Sirk, handing me the box off the back seat.

'Mrs Craigie's finest,' I said with a mouthful, referring to his housekeeper, 'or is there a Mrs Sirk now?'

'No,' he said, ' 'fraid not. Nearly happened once, but then at the last minute I funked it. She was a sweet girl, but I couldn't stop thinking how awful it would be if things turned out wrong and then you were stuck for the rest of your life.' That was just like Sirk, ever the perfectionist.

I said, 'So what do you do for love-life? Still Annie?' That was the housekeeper's beautiful daughter.

'Annie left and got married,' said Sirk dolefully, 'to a chap working in oil in Aberdeen, an American fellow. By now she's probably in Texas, carrying on like those awful people in that thing on the television. But no, I don't do too badly; house-parties and so on you know. At Drumnoch we're not like one

165

of our neighbours – rings a bell fifteen minutes before the gong for breakfast so that everyone can scoot back to their own rooms. But we do try to keep some of the old traditions alive.'

I laughed, and finished the sandwich. 'I'm still hungry,' I complained.

'That's good,' said Sirk. 'We always thought it was best to go in a bit hungry.'

He kicked the low car along fast through the night; there was little traffic and soon we were passing signs for Colchester. Ipswich was less than twenty miles away and I felt a grim, almost joyful anticipation rising in me. I said, 'Supposing the other guys on the barge are straight friends of McMillen's?'

'Good point,' said Sirk. 'In that case we'd better try and lift him, and leave them immobilized. And even if they are all bad boys I don't really think we should just row up to them both in our pea-green boat; we'd be a bit vulnerable. When we get close enough I'll go over the side and climb aboard them astern where I hope they'll not be looking. Then you announce yourself. You could say your friend sent you.'

'You'll swim in the estuary on a February night?'

'Have you ever plunged in a hill loch in August?' said Sirk mildly. 'No? Well, after that, take my word for it, this will be child's play.'

'If they are all bad guys,' I said, 'what's the plan?'

Sirk's eyes left the road for a second to glance at me as he said simply, 'Nobody gets away.'

Chapter 19

It was after one o'clock when we walked out of the woods and on to the mud flats bordering the estuary. It was very cold, but not full dark, with an easterly wind moving low light clouds slowly across the half moon. Sirk gripped my arm. Close to, with the high tide lapping at their sides, three rowing boats were moored to buoys. And to the right, two or three hundred yards across the dark water, out on its own rode the unmistakable bulk of a big sailing barge, the glimmer of ruby and emerald sidelights wavering on the inky surface of the water, and its tall mast, seventy or eighty feet high, with the sails lashed to it.

Without a word we stepped back into the trees; the little wood seemed to be part of somebody's grounds. Sirk was wearing black shoes, dark trousers and a black woollen polo-neck. In the car before we left he had wrapped his pistol in oilcloth and jammed it into his waistband beneath his sweater. I was wearing the shoulder-holster under my jacket, the Browning heavy under my left arm.

'She's a coasting barge, I think,' he said quietly; 'good for punching into the seas of the east coast and the estuary rather than Thames and Medway work. They were generally more shapely and what they called sea-kindly than the others, but the great thing was their shallow draught, only two and a half or three feet when they were unladen, so they could work their way up the inland waterways; there's no keel, just the lee-boards, fan-shaped wooden boards hanging halfway along the sides, to stop them drifting sideways when they're running to windward. They were the last craft to trade under sail.'

'Wonder what they use it for,' I said.

'Yes,' said Sirk, 'if they *are* INLA, at a pinch they could run to Holland, and a picturesque craft like that would be good cover. Or they could rendezvous with other vessels further out. You could move some useful ordnance in a craft that size.'

'But it's so bloody big,' I said. 'The guy said just Frank and O'Connor and another guy were aboard. That wouldn't be enough to sail it, would it?'

'Oh yes,' Sirk said. 'Originally they had a crew of just two – skipper and mate, and that could be his wife. You see they were designed to be handled by the smallest possible crew. They were fine sailormen and strong lads – the mate had to winch that mast up and down on his own, with the sails already hoisted. And the sails are enormous; they're brailed up now, the sprit mainsail and the mizzen behind and the foresail stowed. She'll most likely have an auxiliary diesel motor.'

'OK, OK. Now what's the set-up when we get out there?'

'Well, the steering wheel is set right aft, you can just see the wheelhouse above the rudder there. If there's a man on watch he'll probably be there. On my friend's barge the companionway to below deck was to the left of the wheel, but there may be other arrangements. Once you get below, first of all at the bottom of the companionway there's the cabin where the captain used to sleep, which had a bunk and a folding table and a stove, but it may hold the engine now. That's partitioned off from the main hold and the forehold, which are usually one continuous space, really large, about sixty or seventy foot long and thirty or more wide. Then, forward of that, there's the chain locker and the tiny forehold where the mate slept. Being converted for cruising, the hold will probably have been fitted out for living and some of it partitioned off for cabin spaces. Try to stall them till I appear, but if you can't and if you don't find all three, don't forget the cabins. And don't shoot if you can help it – leave it to me. Are you ready?'

'All right,' I said. I took the Browning from the holster, jacked a round into the chamber, eased the hammer forward again and, putting the safety on, replaced it. For a moment I looked out over the water at the dark shape of the barge. I remembered, suddenly and vividly, Sheila sitting next to me in the lamplight on my bed eating a green apple.

'I'm ready,' I said. 'Let's go.'

The ebb tide was running and we rowed across it, angling towards the barge's dark bulk. It was freezing cold and our bottom halves were soaked and muddy from getting to the boat; and the rowing was hard, though Sirk beside me was evidently an expert and took more than his share. As we drew closer, details emerged; the way the barge hung nose upstream on the anchor chain, the dinghy with an outboard tilted up out of the water riding strung out behind it, the converging pencil lines of the shrouds emerging against the dark sky, the low graceful curve of her deck line. There were no portholes, but beneath the tall masts soft golden illumination shone faintly from narrow lights set in the hatch covers. Fifty or sixty yards away from her, the clacking of our rowlocks as we pulled sounded very loud above the small water sounds and the whine of the wind. Suddenly, incongruously, I caught a whiff of cooking smells, frying, and looking again saw a darker line, a column of smoke pouring from a stove pipe on the deck.

'Late supper is under way,' murmured Sirk, and then, handing me the oar, 'time for my bath,' and the boat wobbled crazily as he slipped to the edge and lowered himself sound-lessly into the icy water and struck out, plunging deeply into the dark. I was the one who made the noise, slapping and catch-ing crabs until I mastered the two oars, by which time I had to struggle to make up the ground I had lost to the tide. It was long minutes before the green light and the barge's stern were looming above me. I could hear the incessant creaking and groaning of her timber. Then a voice came out of the dark from above.

'Who's there?'

My heart pounded. I pulled again until the little boat's side thumped hard against the barge's fan-shaped lee-board and then said, 'Oh, hi. I'm looking for Frank McMillen.'

'Never heard of him.' But I'd already seen astern the wreath name-ribbon incised and white painted on the transom *Hotspur*, so I knew I was at the right place. However, I had a problem: how to secure the rowing-boat to the barge. There was a line in the front of the boat but every time I went to grab it the boat drifted away from the barge's side. I shipped the oars awkwardly and, standing, grabbed the massive lee-board, hoping to tie up to that; but then I heard footsteps hurrying along the deck and simultaneously felt the rowing-boat tugging away from under me. Panicking, I jumped, hauling myself scrabbling up the lee-board and rolling over the low rail on to the sloping, slippery deck. I caught a glimpse over the side of the rowing-boat drifting away in a circle, and then gave my full attention to the man coming towards me; I rolled up into a crouch and straightened with the gun coming out from under my jacket, my arm with it going all the way until it was pointing straight into his face, and three foot from me he saw it and stopped dead.

After a moment he started to bluster.

'My name's O'Connor and I'm the owner of this —'

But I cut him off quietly with, 'The ex-owner, if I get one more word.' That did it. 'All right,' I murmured. 'Now back up.'

We walked together along the edge of the hatch back towards the open-fronted wheelhouse. I concentrated on keeping my balance on the gently undulating slippery deck; the whole thing was on a massive scale, the main mast towering above and the top of the hatch covered with two coils of rope like Cretan mazes and, stowed to one side, long oars, sweeps and boathooks.

We had nearly reached the base of the mizzen mast when there was a noise from a scuttle-hatch with a curved top in front of us. I made one urgent gesture to O'Connor to stay where he was and ducked down beside the main hatch. A head appeared saying, 'What is it, Jimmy?' and then a figure heaved himself up through the hatch. O'Connor could see I had the gun on him and stood motionless by the rail as a third head appeared and a still bulkier figure thrust up on to the deck. And this one I knew.

Slipping off the safety catch and cocking the heavy pistol, I rose, and holding it out in front of me pointed between them at chest height, said tightly, jubilantly, 'Don't move, Frank, or you're dead, motherfucker.'

They all froze, hands going up. I felt on top of everything, invincible again, I had to hold myself back from laughing. I was still doing that when the lightest sound came behind and to my left and it was so sudden and yet so quiet and steady that I was turning more in polite curiosity than alarm when something smashed into the side of my skull and I fell forward into the black.

Chapter 20

The first thing I was aware of was the noise; not just the engine throbbing close by, but the combined continuous creaking of a thousand joints, in the planking of the floor, the barge's sides and the deck above, and intermittently tremendous slamming, clanking noises that I felt reverberate through me. I kept my eyes closed and explored my body; but with my senses, not my hands, as those were tied together, lashed tight to something wooden. My head really throbbed; I felt every slam as it came and I wanted to throw up.

After a while I opened my eyes cautiously. I was lying on cushions on a bench, with my hands tied to a substantial shelf above, on one side of what I guessed was the main hold, a cavernous area lit by a pair of oil lamps swinging on gimbal rings at this end. By the foot of the bench was the companion-way down from the wheelhouse above. The hold was about forty feet long, and interrupted by a massive steel pillar under the mast case. Beyond that a second set of steps rose to the starboard end of the afterhatch. Whoever had surprised me had probably come up on deck that way. The far end under the main hatch was partitioned off into two big cubicles, six feet wide and about twenty long, with a narrow passage between them running to the bulkhead at the sharp end. Despite a pot-bellied stove at this end, the hold was very cold and smelled of salt and damp. Feet were stamping about on the deck above, and shudders ran through the barge as the slamming and clanking continued; I guessed that this was probably the massive rudder kicking, and the lee-boards banging the sides. And then I realized with a shock that the barge was moving; we were under way.

I realized two other things simultaneously: Sirk wasn't there and the second pistol was still stuck in my boot. And then I came to full attention as hobnail boots appeared, clattering down the steps close to my feet. The man descending reached the bottom of the stairs and stood in the swaying lamplight. I saw my Browning in his waistband. It was Frank McMillen.

'You're with us,' he said with a grin, standing over me. 'I thought Casey might have tapped you a wee bit too hard. But your brains must be scrambled already, coming here on your own that way. We've checked the ship for any pals and there's no one. What were you thinking of, coming in that way?'

'Finding out what you had on my friend to make him do those things,' I said.

'Your friend was scum,' said Frank calmly, 'criminal scum who had delusions of political grandeur. And you're just the first half without even the second. You'll not be missed.'

There were footsteps on the companionway and a heavy-set man in seaman's slops with a blue-jowled lantern jaw, small black eyes and a snub of a nose bent down to report to Frank.

'We're making eight knots now; we'll be passin' Harwich in another fifteen minutes. What then?'

'Take her out about a mile and then drop down south towards Walton backwaters. It's a sea of mud and back-channels there, if there's pursuit. And a good place to unload ballast,' he said, jerking a thumb at me. 'But tell Jimmy to keep a good eye out now for the ferry-boats and such like, there's plenty of traffic in the roads. You and Michael stay up there and watch. Come down when Jimmy tells you we're off the backwaters. Don't worry,' he grinned, 'the worst is over – which was getting that bloody big anchor up with the tide against us. When you come down there'll be just light work; that's giving this wee man a rompering he'll be screaming about all the way to hell.'

The second man nodded once, and then his boots clattered up the steps. I stared at Frank's face, scared, but hating him with all my being. From what they said Sirk must have over-estimated himself and bought it in the estuary. My only chance now was to get my hands free. Trying to keep my voice even I

173

said, 'You call me scum. But I never killed anyone just to make a point.'

'You'll never know what it is to believe in anything long enough to forget about saving your own precious hide.'

'Why, is it going to end up like Sheila's did?'

'That was a mistake,' said Frank with what sounded like real regret; 'in a war it happens, and I'm sorry for it. It was down to your friend.'

'And the woman outside the Bailey?' I said.

'Denny again,' said Frank. 'He was always reckless, careless, a hothead; not professional, and never really one of us, however much he wished it, and tried to use us to give his life a direction.'

'Is that why you were doing a Judas job on him to the police?' I sneered and the minute it was out knew I'd made a bad mistake.

Frank's face took on an intense and serious look as he murmured, 'Well, well. Now how did you come to hear about that? I thought you were just another cowboy; you had my number and you'd come to *revenge* your cowboy friend. But there's more to you than meets the eye, little man; and we're going to find out what it is if we have to take you apart to do it.'

I cleared my throat and gestured him to come closer; he bent his head carefully and when it was a couple of feet from mine I spat hard into his face, shouting as he recoiled, 'You're such a fucking heavy hitter, why don't you cut me loose and we'll get to it?'

He didn't bother wiping his face before his left fist blurred in and smacked me in the eye. My head snapped back but I managed to say, 'The cozzers hit harder than you do.'

Frank's glasses glinted as he smiled and tilted his head.

'Oh no – we're going to get to parts of you that the others can't reach. Now here's a taster.' He let me watch the meaty right fist closing. With my hands strung up there was nothing to do. I don't think he meant to put me out, but the force of the punch snapped my head back against the wall, and the light went again.

Cold water exploded in my face and I fluttered my eyes open, or one of them, as the right eye was already mostly closing. The thick-set one, Casey, was standing by the bench, crouched, though there was a full six feet of headroom in the hold, holding a dripping empty saucepan. Behind him, Frank and the third of them, Michael, a wiry younger man with curly black hair were looking down. There were revolvers in their belts.

'We're off the backwaters now and Jimmy'll hold her nice and steady,' said Frank. 'There's nowhere to run, Jack, and no one to hear you scream. It's Question Time in the House.' He grinned at me. 'Untie him, Casey, and bring him to the table.'

The big man bent and began unfastening the ropes. I tensed, waiting for a chance to go for my gun; but as the ropes loosened he had both my wrists clamped firmly in one huge bone-crushing paw, and the third man came forward and grabbed one arm, while Casey shifted his grip to the other one, and they dragged me up. There was nothing calculated about the way I struggled to get free of them; and the awful power-lessness, as they dragged me inexorably towards the table folded down from the opposite wall, drained my strength and my will to resist. With no words spoken they pulled me round so my back was to the wide table; I flashed that they had done this before.

Frank stood in front of me and said, 'Now you can have it quick and easy – answer up and then a dome-job,' he said tapping his forehead and then the Browning; 'or slow and hard, Jack. I'm going to ask you: how did you come to hear about us and Denny and the coppers?'

The sweat broke out on me and I swore at him in the same way I had struggled, just a pure instinctive outpouring of filthy invective. He didn't touch me, just waited till I paused for breath and said, 'Hands, lads.'

One on each side, they bent me back over the wide table

and stretched my arms out on either side; I craned my neck to see Frank pulling a heavy pocket-knife with a cross-hatched black handle from his trouser pockets and struggling to lever open the stiff three-inch marlinspike on it. Casey handed him a similar one and he opened that too. I tried to clench my fists but Michael and Casey clutched the wrists so that as I looked left and right along the table I saw my hands lying on the wood half open, palms upward like stranded crabs. The boat was creaking and the lamps were swaying crazily. I gazed wildly back at Frank, saw him step in, his knuckles whitening around one knife handle with the single long claw of the spike protruding stiffly downwards from his big fist.

He was close to my right hand when he halted, raised his head and his left arm and said, 'A moment, lads.'

We all froze, listening to the noise of the sea, the engine and the wooden craft. Just above our heads there was the sound of something knocking and dragging along the deck.

Frank's head went left and right quickly, listening, calculating.

'We're holding steady,' he said. 'Jimmy must have screwed down the brake on the wheel. He's maybe gone to have a look at something. We'll go up. Michael, stay with him.'

My wrists were released, the dark-haired one stepped back and drew his pistol as Frank and Casey turned away and went in a swift, careful crouch towards the steps to the forward hatch. They passed the massive mastcase and were almost to the foot of the stairs when the hatch above them began to open. They fanned out and pulled their pistols.

'What is it?' cried Frank. 'Jimmy?'

There was thumping above. Legs appeared at the top of the steps. I watched Michael minutely but he was careful, his gaze flashing away from me to the hatch momentarily, always returning, the gun held steady on my chest.

'Jimmy,' said Frank. Then the legs began a slow slide down the steps. More and more came into view. I was aware of a scampering above but my eyes were riveted as I saw Casey and

Frank recoil, mouths open as Jimmy's body, limp and lifeless, bumped into sight feet-first down the steps, a bib of bright blood a foot and a half long down the front of his dark seaman's sweater where his throat had been cut.

Michael looked too, shouting something, and I braced my hands back against the table and lashed out with both feet, catching his hip as he turned back swinging the gun on me; I connected hard and he careered backwards across the floor, arms windmilling, as I ducked, scrabbling for the automatic in my boot; then close by, to the left, from the corner of my eye I saw a dark shape dropping straight down the aft companionway and Sirk landing in a crouch and, one-handed, opened fire.

In the hold's confined space the noise of the Browning was like a bomb detonating. His first bullet hit Michael in the side before he ever recovered balance and cartwheeled him against the far wall, and then a second shot slammed him on to the bunk and he caved in to stillness. I was crouched beneath the table, fumbling the safety off the Walther as I glimpsed Sirk raising his right arm and sighting carefully the forty feet down the length of the hold; I snapped a glance right just in time to see Frank beyond the mast steadying his aim two-handed, and then like rolling thunder the two shots boomed out simultaneously. I saw Sirk double over like a marionette, clutching his left thigh but with the Browning still clamped stubbornly in his right fist. I heard a clatter and saw Frank's pistol go spinning as his gun hand splayed open, rocking back on his heels, his other hand grabbing at his shoulder as he spun round and then disappeared, half falling into the doorway of the left-hand sleeping cubicle. Sirk was down, lying by the stove, and then with a roar big Casey appeared round the left of the mast, ignoring me, revolver coming down on Sirk; and I jerked the Walther up at the big Irishman's face as he came, and fired.

A blur of blood and white splinters flew from his skull as he was hit, staggering, his hands flying to his wounded head; but he was still upright and then coming at me like a ghoul, big, unstoppable, face a mask of red, hands out in front of him stiff and clawed, glistening with his own blood, and I was backing to the bulkhead, standing over Sirk and firing the Walther fast without stopping, the automatic's sharp concussions in the confined space blurred into one deafening wall of noise, bullets firing into the ship's timbers around him leaving bright white splintered scars, or smacking into his body; but still he was coming, fearless, possessed, looming huge and I was yearning desperately for some cannon that would sledge the crazy bastard right down, when I jerked off the last round point-blank into his chest before the empty gun slide locked back, the bullet's impact spraying my face with his blood as I hurled the useless gun at him and at that moment he fell forward, clawing my legs, then bloody fingers convulsing, scrabbling at my boots as he twitched and jerked for long, long moments before his body subsided into stillness.

There was a prolonged pause. The ship heaved and creaked, the diesel throbbed steadily; close to, shiny cartridge cases from the automatics rolled whirring back and forward across the blood-stained floor as the barge pitched on the open waves. Sirk had pulled himself up by the stairs and, ignoring Casey's body, had his gun half raised, fumbling in his pockets for a fresh magazine while his eyes stayed fifty feet away on the door of the port cubicle.

I scrabbled doubled up across the floor to the bunk and scooped up Michael's heavy revolver from where it had fallen, then faced front too as I heard Sirk's flat, quiet voice behind to my right say, 'McMillen's in there, and he's alive.'

I craned forward; I'd just spotted the Browning Frank had carried lying in the passage between the cubicles when gunfire boomed again and I turned to see Sirk's arm track carefully as he sent four spaced shots one after the other ploughing through the thin panelling of the cubicle at regular intervals.

'His gun's on the floor,' I yelled. 'Shall I —'

'No, get him if he comes out,' Sirk said. 'We don't know what —'

We both saw it at the same moment, but only Sirk reacted;

while I was still trying to interpret the blunt snout edging around the cubicle's door, Sirk's raised arm flashed down like lightning and in an instant he fired and saved our lives, hitting McMillen's arm, his stentorian roar of, 'Get DOWN,' bringing a reflex obedience from me in the instant before the blinding flash, the smoke, and the express-train closing sound, and then the unbelievable explosion.

I came to blind, drowning, the salt and icy water masking my eyes, invading my mouth and nose; I was choking, clawing and thrashing for air, only getting further into the chilling water when a hand closed on my collar and pulled me up into the light. I flailed, shaking water from my eyes and head as Sirk dragged me up the aft companionway. The high lamp swung crazily to show me fragments of the scene – in the seconds I had been unconscious the huge hold had filled halfway up with water pouring frothing through the gaping hole McMillen's shoulder-launched rocket had torn in the starboard side. Things were floating on the surface, the bodies of the two Irish gunmen among them. Behind us the diesel hissed and fumed as water engulfed it.

The sea was slapping and sucking at our legs and I scrambled and clawed up the steps of the companionway, but, un-believably, Sirk's hand was restraining me. I screamed at him, my face inches from his, 'Come on! For Christ's sake . . .' but his head never turned, pistol pointing upwards and half extended, his gaze intent for long seconds back across the hold beyond the mast and, as I wildly followed his eyes' direction, sure enough, with the water at our waists, from the port cubicle, past the body of the man called Jimmy came slapping and floating a twice-wounded Frank McMillen. And Sirk's Browning came down, steady, inexorably; a last shot slammed out and beside the mast the top of McMillen's head disinte-grated. His body flopped once and the last glimpse I caught of it was swirling like a bundle of rags away on the flood, and then I had hustled the hobbling Sirk up through the hatch and

179

burst out myself into the madness of the sea-swept night.

The deck was awash and the waves smashing in, over-running the vessel in seconds. I stood paralyzed until Sirk grabbed my arm and shoved me back, splashing round the wheelhouse to the stern, where, as the deck heaved and tilted, his hands worked deftly to unfasten the ropes connecting the dinghy to the transom. The waves were surging round our knees and it was free, Sirk hauling it in and we half jumped, half stepped into the wooden craft, Sirk wincing as he went down heavily on his wounded leg but coming up to scrabble for the motor as I fended us away from the stern of the foundering barge.

Like a sea monster's single eye the green of the starboard light winked out as Sirk brought the motor stuttering into life and swung it down into the choppy water. The blades bit and slowly we edged away from the groaning, sucking roar as the great barge, shrouds flailing, masts tilting, wreathed in boiling foam, slowly and then faster went down into the dark, soon lost to our sight as the waves rose and fell around us.

Sirk had kept the tiller of the outboard all the way, and on a flood of relief to be approaching dry land again I said, 'It's a good thing you know how to work this.'

'I should do – I spent over an hour lying up in it.'

Only then did I realize that must have been how he evaded detection until he had the gunmen where he wanted them and then come over the side and killed the helmsman, despite what could have happened to me in the meantime; but I could scarcely complain, as after that he had saved my life two or three times over.

As we puttered up the estuary and, holding to the right, into the mouth of the Orwell, I remembered Sirk's wound again and offered to take over, but he kept the tiller and we droned on. Cold and drenched, I sank back into the apathetic daze I'd been in since we got clear of the sinking barge. Further on I realized there were a few pinpricks of light, early risers on the southern shore, and the night was draining away to a grey dawn around us. At least the ebb tide had now ceased. We nosed on around the curve of the river, and by the boats where we had taken the rowing-boat Sirk ran the dinghy inshore on the mud of low tide. Then we had to stagger across the flats, each stumbling step an infinite effort in the grey, spurred on by the lightening sky.

Finally we were clear, and reached the trees again. Once there I sank to my knees. I heard Sirk moving behind me and then stop. There were a few birds singing. I found that tears were running down my face, and sobs began to rack my body.

I heard Sirk's voice say, 'Jack . . .' After a while I turned. He was looking at me; he had propped himself up against a tree, deep scarlet streaks on his left leg, face drawn and haggard, grizzled stubble beneath the bristling moustache. Then I saw the butt of the Browning still sticking from his belt. I closed my eyes, then opened them and raised them to his face and said, 'Nobody gets away?'

He stared down at me. I was completely vulnerable in every way then; if he had orders to dispose of me he could have done it with almost my consent. He gave an embarrassed smile.

'There might have been suggestions along those lines in some quarters. But I say,' and his smile broadened wonderfully, 'I say the tidy-minded bastards can all go straight to hell.'

'You're not going to do what they told you to.'

'Never was my strong point. Anyway,' he added hastily, 'if there was anything like that mentioned, I'd say in all that confusion out there,' he nodded back toward the water, 'all that would take care of a lot, wouldn't you think? Only if I were you I should keep a low profile, as they say, for a wee while.'

But I scarcely heard him. Sirk's kindness was the last straw. I started to sob bitterly again. After a moment I felt Sirk's arm around my shoulder and heard him say, 'Jack old boy, what is it? I know you've had a long weekend . . .' I shook my head and sobbed.

'All gone, it's all gone . . .'

'What's all gone, old man?'

'The past, all of it, all my friends; all we wanted and dreamed, all of us.'

'Let it go, old man. I know it's hard, but it's the only way.'

'But they were – they believed things, they really tried. I'm just nothing, a shit, nothing.'

'Nonsense, Jack, you're like most other people.'

'You mean unprincipled.'

'No; easy-going.'

'Yes, but where does the line come between the two?'

'Listen, when it came to it, you did everything you could to help them, to help your friends. As I see it, that's the important bit.'

I had to be content with that. After a while I got up, and it was my turn to support Sirk as we started off through the trees in the first light. Sirk winced, grunted and said, 'First the car and a big pull of malt. Then you drive us to a station and I'll see about telephoning a government quack for this bloody leg of mine.'

Together we hobbled on through the wood.

EPILOGUE

Whatever's written in your heart that's all that matters
You'll find a way to say it all some day
Whatever's written in your heart that's all that matters
Day
Night and day

Gerry Rafferty, Whatever's Written in Your Heart

Lying in a nondescript hotel at King's Lynn, I rested up and took care of the loose ends, paying some dues. Earlier, on the telephone from Blackheath on Sunday evening, I had arranged my way out of England with a guy I had used before. But I had forty-eight hours before the boat he was getting me on to left for Holland, and it gave me time to take care of business. And to think.

There was more sadness, and I knew in the future there would be much more. But now there was a different feeling, too; at the bottom of my tears I felt I might see the attempt to seek the past in its particulars, in the hope that nothing and no one would change, was folly. Release the past, I thought, and like a child or an animal it may come back to you, of its own accord, in its own time, in bright memories and dreams; finally, at the end, it might even make sense. But there's no chasing or forcing it. Better to get on about life's business.

So I did. I had ordered writing paper and stamps and envelopes, and lay on the bed like a lord with a phone on one side and a bottle of Martell and a stack of money on the other, and made my dispositions. I sent £100 to Porky, together with apologies and the location of his bike. I sent my landlady three months' rent and sincere regrets at leaving the attic and at the state she might find it in. I sent Freddy the dentist a big drink and wished him the health to enjoy it. I rang Sid and told him to mobilize the 'erbs and retrieve the Matchless from the Isle of Dogs, if the local talent hadn't already had it away. I rang back later; they'd fetched the bike in a Transit, and I told them they could keep the Gold Star cycle parts if they'd crate up that lion-hearted engine and freight it to a guy I knew in Holland who would fix me up with a new frame and the rest, genuine AMC this time, I was determined. Sid grumbled away but I knew he was going to do it.

There was one last call, and though I was halfway down the

brandy bottle and feeling a lot less pain now, it still made me nervous. When I heard Deborah's sweet voice answer I took a deep breath and said, 'Hi, this here's the Ranking Peanut —'

'Jack!'

'Is Blithers there?' I said hastily.

'No. He's down at the car pound,' she giggled. 'Collecting the van. It seems one of the driver chappies ran off and left it underneath Hyde Park Corner.'

'Dashed impertinence,' I said. 'Listen, I'm sorry about yesterday morning, not being there and all; but stuff happened. If you'll let me, I'll try to make it up to you, if you want.'

'Oh yes,' she said drily.

'Yes. I'm off to foreign parts; points south, eventually. How'd you like to come?'

'How soon?'

'Wednesday. If you say yes, I'll tell you where.'

There was a short pause and then she said, 'When have I ever refused you?'

'Oh Christ, Deborah, I'm so glad . . .'

'Hey, hey, are you sure this is the authentic Peanut? Man of stone? Robot driver extraordinaire? The *Peanut* is happy?'

'Listen, no one loves a smart-ass; you keep this up and I'll have to have some serious second thoughts. I mean a girlfriend with short hair . . .'

'Now, that's more like it; and I suppose I shouldn't tell anyone you called, or where I'm going, or any of that stuff?'

'Tell what? There's nothing to tell. You haven't heard from me, right?'

'Oh, of course. But while you're here, dummy, hadn't you better tell me where you're intending to meet me?'

I told her; we agreed a time and place in Amsterdam and she concluded, 'All I say is, you bloody better be there in Tulip-land.'

'Why?'

'Because you owe me one, remember?'

After she hung up I lay there smiling like an idiot. I had

flirted with the idea of going alone – I'd gone south with a girl before and it hadn't worked out. But then again – I'd gone away alone before, and ended up back where I began. So why not? I was a fool and Deborah, after her fashion, an innocent, and God looks after them both. And in this world in which we find ourselves, I had to suppose that gave us as good a chance as anything else.